FIRESTICKS

American Indian Literature
and Critical Studies Series

Also by Diane Glancy

Poetry
Brown Wolf Leaves the Res
One Age in a Dream
Offering
Iron Woman
Lone Dog's Winter Count
The West Pole

Fiction
Trigger Dance

Nonfiction
Claiming Breath

FIRESTICKS
A Collection of Stories

by
Diane Glancy

University of Oklahoma Press
Norman

"The First Indian Pilot" first appeared in *Farmer's Market* 8, no. 1 (Spring/Summer 1991):87; and *Stiller's Pond* (Minneapolis: New Rivers Press, 1991). "An American Proverb" will appear in an upcoming volume of *The Fiction Review*. "Chelly Repp" first appeared in *Emrys Journal* 1 (1984):87.

Library of Congress Cataloging-in-Publication Data

Glancy, Diane.
    Firesticks : a collection of stories / by Diane
Glancy.—1st ed.
       p. cm. — (American Indian literature and critical
studies series ; v. 5)
    ISBN 978-0-8061-8643-6 (paper)
    1. Indians of North America—Mixed descent—
Fiction. I. Title. II. Series.
PS3557.L294F57   1993
813'.54—dc20   92-35514
                                     CIP

Firesticks is Volume 5 in the American Indian Literature and Critical Studies Series.

The paper in this book meets the guidelines for permanence and durability of the Committee on Production Guidelines for Book Longevity of the Council on Library Resources, Inc. ∞

Contents

FIRESTICKS

THE FIRST INDIAN PILOT

The second world was a black wool blanket. Black as the iron skillet. Greased. Corn popping from the skillet like white stars pinned to the air over the black wool earth.

"Put the lid on, NOW!" Grandmother said. The old grandmother, not the young one. The old women lived so long, a house could have two grandmothers easy. Louis watched her dress that hung longer in front. The apron tied to her rubbery waist.

In their house the nephews were old as the uncles. Barefoot and cruel. Poking one another into trouble.

The black wool earth seemed to move in the distance. The sameness of the night was easy for Louis. He was colorblind. He also had poor eyesight and his eyes would not stand still. Even after eye-surgery they jumped like corn in the skillet he thought.

The far lights of Oklahoma City were not connected with the earth. Maybe that was the way the earth looked from a plane at night. Louis watched the earth, soft and moving from the bodies under it. He wanted to fly the planes he heard from Tinker Air Force base. But no Indian was a pilot. His brothers told him that. No Indian was anything but in the way. A leftover walking in two worlds.

What else could they do? They could live in the second world Louis saw from the window. But he didn't want that. They could live in the first world, the old one, distant and alien to him. He'd really only heard stories which lived sometimes in his head when his grandmothers talked. Or they could walk in that floorless space between two worlds. One foot in each world with those violent eruptions he heard sometimes between his mother and grandmothers, his mother and brothers.

The popcorn had a sound of a jet in the distance. Louis straddled the window-sill and lifted his arms. "Arrrrmmmmmmmm." He mimicked the sound he heard during the day when he sat in the dirt yard and watched the planes rise from the flat earth.

He couldn't fly anyway. Ye ho. His eyes rattled back and forth. His brothers looked at one another and laughed. Then the girls laughed. They were grass-hoppers. Something to chase when they got older. Their faded jeans and shirts pale as popcorn under the lid of the skillet.

Monochromatic.

Louis remembered the word he'd heard at the hospital. Why didn't they just staple his eyelids closed like the screen to the opening in the window? But even it ripped out. Because he sat on the windowsill all the time his old grandmother nagged.

"You know that screen needs to be nailed closed again," she said to Louis, shaking the skillet and swatting at a fly.

No it didn't. How else would the cat get in? The flies like burnt kernels from the bottom of the skillet?

They were all packed into that small frame house between Oklahoma City and Okemah. Even though it was dark, the heat of the day stayed in the house. He had to have the openness of the window. The flat Oklahoma sky ruffed its blackness over him at night. The popcorn still pecked like hard rain during spring storms.

Louis sat in the window and pretended he was a pilot. All the while his old grandmother made popcorn for his nephews and the brothers that were still around. Louis had scratch marks on his legs from the torn edge of the screen. "Tsoo. Tsoo." He shot at the little birds that must be asleep in the bush. He shot at the water-dish his grandmother left in the dirt yard. He could see it shining in the light from the window.

He looked up at the stars. The Coma Berenices. The constellation he learned about. Didn't pilots navigate from the stars? The constellation was also called Berenice's Hair. He looked for the white fuzz in the sky, but the stars were jerking around in their orbits and he couldn't tell. Just like his dizziness. They said it came from his eyes.

Louis read the constellation book after school while his teacher graded papers. When his eyes jumped and he couldn't read any longer, she read the words for him. Then there were tutors and the other people who came to school. He liked the ones who played the banjo and guitar.

The voice of his nephews and brothers popped in the kitchen and he looked at them. They were fighting over the bowl of popcorn, pulling it back and forth. "AYYYYheyy," he lifted the bowl from the table until they kept their arms out of the way and took the kernels with their hands. The bowl was almost empty. The old grandmother went to the wood-stove. Louis held the bowl on the table while the nephews and brothers finished.

All of them could see what he couldn't. He had memorized the colorwheel. Blue. Yellow. Red.

What were they? He had asked. But no one knew what to say.

The colorwheel made things look the way they did, and he didn't understand. Light or dark but he knew that. Maybe it was the way the banjo was different from the guitar. Or something like the difference in the scale. Maybe the spectrum of color had a similarity to the music he heard at school.

Blue. Yellow. Red.

Were they like the different notes? Not well played sometimes.

What was color like? It came through the eyes. He knew that.

The new corn popped in the skillet. He lifted the lid when the old grandmother wasn't looking. It was pure as a spirit leaping from its body. Sometimes he could forget his eyes and fly. But then the night felt black again when his eyes got to jerking. A blackbody. Something that absorbed all light falling on it without giving back any reflection. His oldest brother had a curtain of it at his window so he could sleep in the day. Once he had a night job as a janitor, but now he just drank into the dawn. No Indian was anything.

"Here, get that lid on the skillet!" His old grandmother harped. Some of the corn shot from the black skillet like parachutes over the edge of the stove. The nephews jumped down from the table and picked the corn off the floor. It was puffy as the old grandmother's feet in their dirty house-shoes. She clucked her tongue at them. But he saw her eat the fallen pieces too.

The corn in the large skillet seemed to lose its popping and the old grandmother got a twig from the kindling he had piled in the corner of the room. None of the older brothers would help. They were lost in the second world. He memorized the colors they all saw but him.

Blue. Blue-green. Green.
Yellow. Yellow-red. Red.

He held the colorwheel in his hand. An orbit the earth followed on its way past the Coma Berenices?

If he were a girl he would get off easier. Girls were never colorblind. They just carried it for their sons.

He wanted to be anything but the youngest of the uncles. All the evils of the olders rolled onto him. The buffalo wallows that caught the runoff. Only he did not want the rain he felt sometimes behind his eyes. The grandfathers were all dead. The fathers gone to New Mexico or Los Angeles. They'd be in the dirt yard one afternoon and gone the next. Sometimes he could hardly remember them. Maybe they got tired of having nothing to do and fled to barrooms and the rows of beds in missions. The boyfriends of the nieces still came around, but they too would disappear like the colors he didn't know.

Now the corn had a sound of a low backfiring. One of the older brothers when he went off to drink in Oklahoma City or Okemah. The eruption of the neighbor's dog when the cat wandered into his yard. The growl of heat-thunder that woke him sometimes.

"What color is the kitchen?" Louis asked.

"I can't remember what it used to be," the old grandmother said. She had grease on her fingers from oiling the skillet for more corn. Little salt-beads staked her fingers. The colors got harder. He had read them.

Vermilion. Manganese. Sienna.

What were they? Parts of other colors? The sound of guitar and banjo playing different songs. Maybe an Indian flute.

He asked about the pile of kindling in the corner of the kitchen. He had gathered it for her. She said it was brown but that wasn't on the colorwheel. Was there also a first and second world with color?

He knew it was a brightness he didn't see. Little sparks that came from cans and jars and the torn shirts of his nephews when they got in fights at school. And the tube his mother put on her mouth when she went out.

A sort of light that things carried.

He knew it was a combination of things. The sound of the cat when the old grandmother stepped on its paw. The buzz of flies. The nephews fighting over the new popcorn in the bowl. The grandmother clucking.

But not separate. Not one at a time. But all had their own way of sounding together. All had their way of sounding out their own kind of light.

The land was greased. It was enough to pop them like corn. Mid-August, they couldn't walk on the pavement without jumping. Even after dark, Louis could feel the heat rise from the postage-stamp yard as he sat in the window. Wasn't his race popped off the earth? Weren't they unwanted? Where could they go? Follow the grandfathers into the black and white sky at night? The first world was gone and the second world had come to take its place.

But he couldn't see it like it was. The second world looked black to him with flat, white stars nailed to the air. He wanted to call back the old earth. The first one.

Yo!!

For a moment something flashed in his eye. A falling star. A gist of what could be color. A slash of something other than what was?

Louis rubbed his sore eye like the bubble a pilot pulled over the cockpit.

Something flashed and Louis reached for it again. It was like the sound of a story or the moving tribe. It was something he couldn't quite understand.

He reached from the window and stepped from the second world up.

JACK WILSON
OR WOVOKA
AND CHRIST
MY LORD

Native American heritage is something I don't like
to get into. You see I have as much white blood as
red. I shouldn't be talking but it's hard to be quiet.
Not really that either because it was years before I
started saying what I thought. The fact that I had
opinions that mattered took me from Oklahoma to
Minnesota to realize.

I remember in school being small and brown.
Someone would mention the freckles on my face.
Pecan-Face would have been my Indian name if I
had one. I also knew my hide was transparent. It's
true though no one told me to my face. It's one of
those things you just know. Every feeling I ever had
showed. I remember my face burning in class with
shame. I think it was because of my Indian heritage.
I think it's influenced everything I do. Yet I'm also
white. I want you to remember that.

Now this is what I have against Indians. I don't think they care for the land they say they care for. I think they're irresponsible. They only care about their good times. High hooters. Rooty fluters. Ghosters. Who thought they could chase away the white man. Thought they could call back buffalo. Thought they could return the ancestors. Handle firewater. Handle a bigger than.

Oh I know, be generous. Their culture was ripped off, then they're expected to be kind to the earth. We expect them to do more with less.

We had a Native American Awareness week at our college and I invited a speaker. This Indian poet dude. I saw right away I was invisible to him. Women are short-skirters or nothing to the accou- trements in his head. His attitude you see. Warrior and squaw. I saw him look at all the girls.

On the phone he had told me how he had dried out and I thought he would be a good speaker for the students and maybe he had you see but not enough to know in the meantime I raised the children took the warbonnet raised the tomahawk and went after the great reservation nothingness that licked us up and down and all over just when it wanted to. And he read about his warrior sons when he had no children. Had not been a father. Said his own father left him and his stepfather beat him and he had a hundred reasons and I'm sure all true but he annoyed me with his superior-ass stance in front of everyone. And I the one who invited him was invisible too.

I sat there on the front row thinking I mattered too. I remembered the time I walked down the road on the old place and a bird sang on a wire. Someone said don't you hear what that bird is saying and you know I did. I don't know exactly what in words but in his language he said I was visible in the invisibility I would feel. I knew already what he meant.

So the bird had told me I was pretty but not in the meaning you think of. Not exactly spiritual either. But in presence. Substance. That something visible. So while the poet looked at a young girl and asked to be kissing cousins, asked almost in front of everyone to touch her sweet brown hide and I the one who invited him remembered what the bird had said while I listened to the Indian guy say he wanted to be a teacher because girls wore short skirts. And I thought that's an Indian for you. Or maybe just a man. And I thought what tough-guy learned responses that he maybe didn't even think about but that's the way he was the old way and that's how he would be.

I believe in being generous up to a point and then I think to say things like they are.

Well you have that buck warrior probably promising more than he could deliver up there jabbering about his life and his firewater fleamarket days along the bar-rails of life and I thought this is the heritage I received from my forefathers? This is the message we pass to the young? Like it was a piece of licorice or a black snake twirling up our leg. Well he'd had a good time at least til it caught up with him.

While I was given by the just God the role of wife
mother the other lesser not mattering one. I was
given myself to be responsible. Not a card-carrying
Indian. Not a card-carrying White. But school-
teacher, provider, minority, and everything nobody
else wanted to be. An Indian because I wasn't
White. An Indian because I could synthesize the
fragments and live with hurt. Yipes.

Me and all the runny-nosed reservation children
suffering alcoholism poverty want closed-minded-
ness growing up to engender the same in their own.

I'm getting rid of my grumpiness.

But it was in church this white guy minister funda-
mentalist who ran his church like a battleship and
allowed no women on his pews without a hat this
very opposite of the Indian dude said Christ made
us whole well we could walk over any pitfall and
not fall or if by strange chance we fell of our own
accord you see not his of course Christ's that we
could get up rise to our feet and go on as if we
hadn't fallen at all and I thought I wanted to be able
to do that so I went to the altar without making a
sound while everyone else was howling Jesus like
the baboon in the zoo in Tulsa and I wanted to go on
by myself without anyone holding me up you know
by the shirt collar or ankle straps or shoestrings on
my keds and well it worked I just went on through
my life praising Jesus and raising my communion
cup to him saying glory hallelujah being now
another bird myself on the wire on the old place
giving out words of life that would last through all

the days and would usher into the hereafter as if it were a cool theater on a hot Oklahoma day and the nickel to get in was Christ and you had it too and all that mattered was you and he.

It probably wouldn't work for everyone. In the end it may not matter. God may not care what he is called whether male or female because he is spirit and in the hereafter we are neither either.

Yet I still think there will be intercourse. Does not Christ do all this talk about his longing for his bride? I maybe be straying but there's some sort of fucking we're not accustomed to yet, but will grow to like, I'm sure. You know how that's supposed to be and in the end really it turns out all right because you end up wanting it about the time he doesn't.

And the Indian intellectuals write their surreal coyote tales. He is now she eating at trendy restaurants wearing high-top tennies and who knows what. The changing surviving ole Coyote finally teaches in the end that there's no ultimate reality no foundation and whatever he/she believes is true and the "heesh" eats away at the foundation the thought there is anything solid like the Rock of Ages under our feet. Well he denies that final authority yes he does and is proud of it.

We had another speaker at Native American week who told stories that didn't have a lot to do with what we would call ordinary life and he probably had the same attitudes as the other dude just hid them off better but he told a story of prophecy of how the white man would come and use up even the stars. But one star was saved for us and he snapped a cottonwood twig right in two and there was a star something the way you cut an apple crossways and there's a star just our slice of heaven right there in an apple.

And he told this story although it was a story that could only be told when there's snow on the ground. But you know they'd had a sweat and prayed that morning and it snowed that very hour yes it did and he talked about Indian spirituality and how it called snow down from the heavens but what happened still in the rest of the world the hunger disease injustice he could do nothing about but we had snow that morning and he told the story. This other world in the midst of our own dark one. A star from another place and it was ours yes because we held the broken twig of cottonwood in our hand.

I don't know why my white husband was surprised that I wanted a divorce there were times I started crying and couldn't stop. Yet I didn't want to be without that support invisible as it was from time to time most of the time really if I'd look at it with square eyes. But once you have children if he's willing to stay you usually let him empty as the house is even with him in it. We never had enough of the other and just burrowed into ourselves. This living is just surprising isn't it? The absoluteness of it you see no matter what Coyote says.

Yet you know somewhere say Tucumcari there's this Indian dude riding down the street with his easy-rider cycle his headband and black silky hair streaming like crows in the night air or black fish deep in the river and he's about as stable as that April snowfall but you look at him anyway and say that's part of my heritage. It's nothing you can stand on no nor even put your finger on but it sure does make a show.

Yet he's so full of metal he couldn't get through the detector-booth in an airport. Can't fly really so heavy with his heritage but I remember sitting on a runway once in a plane looking through the little opening that's supposed to be a window and I saw a plane rushing ahead of us on the runway to take off lifting in that exhaust smoke and noise and jittering our own plane on the runway behind it as it lifted there right in the air ahead of us like a cross with its arms outstretched.

THE CROSSWALK AT GALTIER PARK

It was a mail run to Minneapolis.
The prairie highway fishtailed through the hills.
The glad hands
running on eighteen donuts.
Whad you expect? The last time he was at his
girlfriend's house. She seemed surprised. If
someone was there, he made his escape out the
backdoor.

The speed limit around her was two nickels.
Put it in grandma.
Set it down.
Woo.
He was the tailboard artist.
Or a nearly perfect driver.
Okie Padoke.

He went to the Povlitzki's Cow Palace with her on
Friday nights when he got back from his run.
Tired out
still roaring after several one thousand miles
the place sank into him.

Why'd he put those lights all over his truck like
tattoos?
You have pictures on the wall of your house
don't you? Well he had to carry his with him.

She's got a wide spread.
He said things like that when everyone was
listening. His girl was dancing with another guy
or one of her girlfriends. The two-step.
Variations he didn't know.

He was glad to be with her. It was better than
wolfing it in some all nighter.
Chuz. He downshifted in his chair.

She could be his swamper anytime
riding with him.
Until he passed some sheepherder on the road.
Started back south again with the next load.

Povlitzki's shifted to high gear.
He liked Friday nights. The red walls,
the steerhorns over the bar, pulltabs,
an old Christmas tree left in the corner
its lights blinking like an oncoming truck,
the noise.
It was after-Christmas after all
he remembered.
That feeling of an uphill-drag was always with him.

The bandstand was lighted as a truck-stop.
The drums had rings around Venus. Or was it
Saturn?

When he was on the road he watched the sky.
The stars turning above him,
the white moon-face of the drum.

But at Povlitzki's he was back on earth.
The row of horses on a shelf reminded him.
The ropes, lassos. His girl laughing.
The dart board, pool table. Everything you'd want.

But the road was what he longed for.
There was a boy he always saw on the crosswalk
at Galtier Park
giving him the hand-signal to honk.
Sitting above the traffic watching it go by
knowing there was someone wanting to go
with him.
Someone thinking he was something.

Didn't the boy know what the road was like? He
deserved more than waving from crosswalks. He
deserved more than windshield wipers waving
in his face
and a field of sleet under his wheels.
Doaker. Soaker. Next time he'd be well below the
weight.

He watched his girl
with her arms around another man
on the dance-floor.
What did she matter? He had several women after
him. Some in Mexican overdrive.

The music pounded like his truck. He had his own
beat on the road he danced to. She couldn't
understand.

Povlitzki's was smokey as the highway on a dusty
night.
He could jam her anytime.

Bucky Buck. That was his handle.
He could feel the steering wheel in his hands.

What a way to ruin a relationship.
He heard from the next table.
Getting married.

Well it was always women.
Who cared if he couldn't dance
the way she wanted?
Yes he was ready for his next run.

Wasn't Christmas about a journey,
a travel to another place?

But it was the thought of her he took with him.
The guy on the motorcycle
might be turning in her drive before he got to the
crosswalk where the highway turned south.
They might already be grinding their gears.
Yug.
A woman with two hearts.

He tapped his foot to the drum
and held his thumb up to the stained ceiling at
Povlitzki's.
He remembered fishing on the lake once long ago.
Rain hitting the water make little tongues jump up
from the lake.
The little drops of rain falling were also tongues.

Tongues licking tongues.
Shit. He would make sure all lights were burning
on the racks.

Some cement-mixer would be behind him. He could
almost hear the engine coming.

And what of all the sleeping farms he passed
in the night?

Trucks were old buffalo herds
their eyes red as a string of chili lights.
All of them straining over the road.

And she was some aviator speeding past.
Maybe he'd give her her flying orders.
Next time he'd think about it anyway.

No he wouldn't.
It was the woman who was his cab-lights,
the moving constellations of the highway.
Yes it was the woman who drove him
into the cold little field of the heart.

FIRESTICKS

"How far did you say it was to Frederick?"

"About three hours."

"I thought you said it was a long trip."

"It is."

"You don't ever get out of Guthrie, Oklahoma?"

"Not unless the woman calls who takes care of my father."

"What's wrong with him?"

"A number of things. He's old and never took care of himself. Usually I take the bus from Guthrie to Frederick."

"I was going south anyway."

"Frederick is just a few miles from Texas."

"Yahoo. That's where I'm headed."

"I thought so."

"I told you I was going there last night in the Diner."

"Yeah, I knew before you told me."

"How?"

"I thought you looked like a dude when I first saw you."

"What does that mean?"

"Someone who moves around. Eats his meals in diners. Sleeps on the prairie. A leftover cowboy."

"You're generous."

"I'm not through. They like nothing better than a free meal and a first-nighter. I've seen a thousand of them."

"All in Guthrie?"

"Yes."

"What difference does it make? The first night or the thousandth?"

"With me it won't be the first night, nor the thousandth."

"You're tough, Turley."

"Turle. Turle Heppner. I told you that last night in the Diner too."

"If I get your name right, will you sleep with me?"

"No."

"What makes you think that's what I want?"

"Most men do. Second to a free meal."

"You don't know my name either."

"How do you know?"

"You weren't paying attention when I told you."

"I was busy. The Diner was packed."

"Does everybody get paid on Friday nights in Guthrie?"

"I don't know. At least they come to eat. But we're busy most every night."

"Navorn."

"Your name?"

"Yes."

"Something like tavern?"

"If you can remember it that way."

"I can."

"And your name is Turle Heppner."

"My father is William Bear Hall. My mother's name was Effie, and my grandmother's name was Jean Lewis Hall. Is there anything else I can tell you?"

"Bear?"

"He's Cherokeee. Partly anyway."

"Why isn't your last name Hall?"

"I was married once."

"A man-hater like you?"

"It only lasted eighteen months, and it was a long time ago."

"You chewed him up and spit him out?"

"Nearly."

"The open road. That's what I like. Second to a free meal."

"I like Oklahoma. We lived in Kansas City when I was born, but we moved to Guthrie before I finished school. My father moved a lot. My mother didn't always go with him."

"I've always lived in one place."

"Where?"

"Wisconsin."

"I thought you sounded different."

"I sold my five forties near the Oconto River."

"Five forties?"

"An eighth of a mile. A place I had."

"Did you have a wife?"

"Yes, but that was a long time ago."

"Children?"

"Yes."

"How many?"

"One."

"Where is he?"

"She. With her mother."

"Where in Wisconsin?"

"Oconto."

"That's an Indian name?"

"Yes."

"We have names like Okemah, Wetumka, Wewoka."

"They sound the same to me."

"You're not used to Indian names."

"You are?"

"We don't have anything called 'Oconto' around here."

"You wouldn't be one of them, would you?"

"What makes you ask?"

"Your dark hair. Your look."

"I am. I told you my father was. Part."

"I'm an eighth."

"How much is that?"

"Out of my eight great-grandparents, only one was Indian."

"That's not much."

"No, it's not."

"About a toe's worth."

"Maybe a leg."

"I noticed you first because of your simple beauty. You don't need paint."

"How old are you?"

"I'll be forty in January."

"That's old to start off as a dude."

"How old are you?"

"Forty-two."

"You're not."

"I am."

"You don't look it."

"But I am."

"I thought Indian women got old fast."

"My father is sixty-two and his hair is still black. Not all Indians age fast."

"I guess not."

"Why did you sell your place?"

"I wanted to leave Wisconsin. I'd never been anyplace else."

"Why did you come to Oklahoma?"

"I didn't. I was just passing, on my way to Texas, I told you. I've been on the road a while traveling around."

"How long?"

"About two years."

"That's a long time to get to Texas. Where have you been?"

"The Dakotas. Nevada. Wyoming."

"Just doing what you feel like doing?"

"That's about it."

"That's what my father always did."

"Now I'm heading south. Picking up waitresses. Taking them to their father in Frederick."

"And to think I offered to pay gas."

"I refused, didn't I?"

"Only because you were going that way. And only because I said I'd pay half."

"You can pay all if you want."

"I don't want to. You have more money than I do."

"Why do you say that?"

"You sold your place in Wisconsin, didn't you? I haven't ever had a place to sell."

"That was a long time ago. I've been on the road a while."

"Not working?"

"No."

"A drifter. A dude. I've served hash to a thousand of them."

"All in Guthrie."

A FAMILY TO WHICH NOTHING HAPPENED

We weren't allowed to have accidents. Things only happened to others. A neighbor four houses down the street was run over by his truck. The brake gave way just as he walked in front of it and he was left paralyzed from the waist down. Across the street a boy with rheumatic fever sat on his porch for what seemed our whole childhood. Several houses up from him a man left his wife and two children. In those days when the wife didn't work it was like clamping off their air.

My friend, Linda Elson, and I visited Mr. Scofield, the paralyzed man. In his house he accused his wife of going to see the barber. You've got a boyfriend he said to her. Over and over in front of us. She stood at the stove.

Sometimes Mr. Scofield tried to get Linda to kiss him. Never me. Things only happened to others.

He'd coax her to come to him. Just touch me, he said, but she wouldn't.

I don't think my mother ever visited the Scofields. She stayed in our house or visited Linda's mother before her father died. Once something happened she didn't go back. She visited the woman next door whose husband delivered mail and had two sisters who weren't married. My first plane trip was to visit the sisters in Evansville, Indiana. They hovered over me for a week then my parents came.

Misery was always confined to other houses. My mother's first lesson was that we were middle-of-the-road people. We lived in Kansas City, Missouri, in the middle of America and we were together for a while in the middle of the country.

If anyone in our family died, it was because they were old. If anyone got sick it was probably because they did something they shouldn't have. My mother's letters to her sister were always that things were the same. War tornado famine blizzard earthquake sucked the world but never at our house or yard.

Not even polio came near. My brother and I waited in front of Woolworth's Dimestore in downtown Kansas City because polio was there. We stood on the curb with our father while our mother went inside.

My mother and father even pinned my brother and me in our beds at night so we wouldn't kick off the covers and get cold. They didn't tell us stories or read us books in which things happened. We slept like little mummies in our beds.

In the afternoons when the weather was warm I sat under the large elm at the curb and watched the samaras flutter down like angel eyes. Only others were left to the ravages that stalked the earth, never us.

There were times when things nearly happened. My father worked for the stockyards. He and the other foremen loaded trucks when the union wouldn't. They broke picket lines and got the work done.

One night during the strike a car stopped in front of our house. My mother saw it from her dark window. But the car drove on. Later that night another foreman's house was bombed. Never ours. I was always safe in my middle-of-the-road bed.

Meanwhile the woman and her two children across the street disappeared somewhere. Probably to a death camp outside Kansas City where they took unwanted women and their children. I remember walking to Dabner's grocer on the corner before they left. I bought the two kids candy with my allowance. Those pastel pinkyellowblue dots stuck to a strip of white glossy paper. Wow. Those candy button strips. Until my father told me not to. My father was even a scout leader passing summers somewhere at a camp with my brother. Leaving my mother and me eating mashed potatoes in her kitchen white as an envelope.

It was a stifling nothing that happened. My mother always seemed angry. I think it was because nothing happened. I don't remember her visit to my campfire girls or sunday school. She took care of the house and that was that.

But she knew that somewhere something happened. Down in the stockyards the cattle marched up the chute to their death and men struggled for their lives. But not in our house. And every evening when my father came home my mother asked him in front of us what happened in the stockyards that day where men filled out orders for new knives and aprons when the old knives were dull from cutting bone and the aprons stained with blood. Where he could hear the wails of the cattle when they smelled death at the end of the chute and the carts of their tongues and hooves and intestines went by and men passed in their aprons and white coats their heavy work shoes and overalls smelled of cows and excrement and blood and death.

I always thought of Mr. Scofield when I heard my mother ask my father, but their drama was unthinkable in our house. It was simply a matter of my father witnessing something happening and my mother wheedling it out of him, purging him of it before it spread to the whole house.

And what did Mr. and Mrs. Scofield do all day while we were at school? Herded into our own little death camps where everything was scrubbed and sorted and the elm leaves and their angel-eye-seeds were pinned on the bulletin board, the eyes staring back. And what did the rheumatic boy do on his porch all day? And Linda Elson's mother without Linda's father, after he died suddenly of his heart attack while my father's heart beat steadily on?

When I was in fifth grade we moved from Kansas City to Indianapolis where my father was transferred to another stockyard. Our furniture and belongings boxed and loaded neatly in a van. My brother and I wrapped in our coats in the backseat of the '49 Ford.

We drove away from the house where I'd lived since I was born. We left Woodland Avenue where 50th Terrace runs up the hill from Paseo and behind us houses rose to Frances Willard School up Michigan and Euclid and other streets whose names I can't remember.

My mother's feet pushed against the floorboard of the car all the way across Missouri and Illinois and Indiana. I sat in the backseat thinking maybe this was an exit, a way out, a move to someplace where finally we would be worthy of something happening to us.

FIRESTICKS

"Where are we?"

"Somewhere on the prairie past Oklahoma City."

"I slept through the city?"

"Yep. You were out."

"We're probably half way to Chickasha. Have we stopped at a toll booth yet?"

"We haven't stopped anywhere. It was nothing to get through the city. Highway all the way. What woke you?"

"A dream I have sometimes. I always see a man, his gray beard dancing like tinsel."

"Is it Christmas?"

"Now that's what's wrong with dudes. They can't think figuratively."

"Look at those hills. They remind me of Girl Scout cookies."

"Are you hungry?"

"What makes you ask that?"

"Maybe because I wait tables and that's usually what I talk about."

"The Barbed Wire Diner. I remember the sign when I drove into Guthrie."

"I think all the Girl Scouts in Guthrie knock on my door."

"Guthrie would be in bad shape without you."

"What have we passed so far?"

"I don't know. All the towns are off the turnpike in Oklahoma. I haven't seen anything but prairie."

"I know a diner in Chickasha that has the best burgers I've eaten."

"Want to stop?"

"It's where the bus always stops. Don't you?"

"Are you going to buy my lunch?"

"Why?"

"I'm taking you to Frederick."

"I'm paying half the gas. You were going this way anyway. I can't stand a man who sponges off a woman."

"Will we sit at the same table?"

"We aren't even to a toll booth yet. There's several of them before Chickasha."

"Tell me about your father."

"I will see my grandmother's face. He reminds me of the way she used to look. The few times I saw her."

"That sign said, 'Chickasha 20 miles.' Did you see it?"

"Yes. Here's your toll booth. Are you going to pay?"

"No. You were coming this way anyway."

"But I'm going farther west than I would have

without you. I was going to take 35 south to Dallas. Now I'll be headed toward Wichita Falls. I looked at the map."

"I'm not paying."

"Damn. Eighty-five cents."

"The others are less."

"You're quiet all of a sudden."

"I'm remembering my Indian grandmother the few times I traveled to visit her house near Hulbert, Oklahoma. I was thirteen when she died. My mother said she must have given up after she broke her hip. But when I visited her grave, years later, I noticed she was seventy-five when she died. All that comes back to me is the coarse hair pulled back under her head, the prominent cheekbones, and the long, hollow body under the covers as she lay quietly in bed. I wish I knew her better, but she was sixty-two, and far away, before I was even born."

"That's the most you've said in one spell."

"I don't think she was ever in our house in Kansas City. My parents were married a long time before I was born. Her visits were terminated before I came."

"Yeah, families can be sticky. Get your feet off the dash."

"I suppose so."

"Why did your grandmother stop coming to your parents' house?"

"I guess because there wasn't much purpose in her visits. No one had anything to say to each other. She and my mother sure didn't have much to talk about. It's not that they fought. They didn't have anything in common. My grandmother didn't say much. I guess it was a strain on my mother to make conversation. She finally wouldn't do it anymore. We only went to see her a few times that I can remember."

"Your grandmother was Indian too?"

"Yes, half. My Cherokee great-grandfather married a white woman after the Civil War. My father is a fourth and I'm an eighth."

"One great-grandparent out of eight."

"She still speaks to me in a voice I can hear. It's as though what she had to say to me passed between us without speaking. I remember her on the bed. I don't remember that she ever said anything. In fact, I remember that she didn't say anything. And yet, something that I'm not sure of passed between us."

"You Indians got some strange stories."

"I'm struggling for a language that would separate us. If I could have heard her, we would have parted like the people after Babel. I might not have liked, nor understood what she said. I would have had a chance to reject it. But we are together in our one language of silence. If she could speak, we would have separated."

"I don't understand what you're talking about."

"Dudes never do."

"What did this guy do to you that you're so bitter?"

"What guy?"

"Your husband."

"He wasn't my husband long enough for me to remember."

"You just knew right away you wouldn't like it?"

"That's right. I worked while he slept. It didn't take me too long to decide."

"Why doesn't your mother come to see your father?"

"She's dead. Whenever I see my father, it's always my grandmother's face I see. My father's lost weight. His cheekbones stand out. I only saw my grandmother a few times in my life and she died nearly thirty years ago. In her face was probably her father's before her. I wasn't close to my father's side of my family. My mother raised me, yet it's his family I feel on windy days when the dust is up. In the red sumac groves I see the circle of their council fires."

"I think of my daughter sometimes too."

"How long has it been since you've seen her?"

"About four years."

"How old is she?"

"I think she's six."

"The hamburger stand is coming up. Right after this next toll booth."

"Sixty-five cents."

"The place has bus seats for chairs. Even a floor furnace like the Diner."

"Another toll booth."

"Sixty-five cents."

"Damn. Are you going to pay?"

"No. I'm going to tell you how to get to Frederick."

"What are those hills?"

"The Wichita Mountains."

"There's mountains in Oklahoma?"

"Yes."

"Those aren't mountains."

"After the toll gate at the end of the Bailey Turnpike, where we are now, turn on Highway 36, then Highway 5 into Tillman County."

"Is that how Oklahoma makes its money?"

"Lawton is that town you see off there."

"It's a long way to Frederick."

"I told you it was. I always wanted to stop at that abandoned house. I see it from the bus window."

"There's snakes in abandoned houses. I'm not stopping. Why's your father in Frederick?"

"It's where he was when he came to the end of his trail. He was in Wichita Falls the last I knew, then I got a call from some woman in Frederick saying she had my father at her house and he was sick. I drove Edward's car once, but I don't like to drive. I get sleepy sometimes. The Diner wears me out. I'd rather take the bus."

"Who's Edward?"

"The man who owns the Diner. There's an antique store for you. Smith's on the edge of town."

"Where are we?"

"Nearly to Frederick. I see it from the bus too. Hinges, rusty tools, yokes, church pew, glass bottles, dentist chair, bathtubs on feet. All the stuff our lives are made of."

"A church what?"

"Church pew. If you went to church more often you'd know what I was talking about."

"I didn't understand you. Did the bus driver stop there for you?"

"No. I looked at all the stuff in the yard as we

passed. I'd have an antique store if I could afford it.
I've always wanted to stop there too."

"Maybe if you'd paid some of the toll."

"Turn here. It's a brick house on Kiowa and
North Twelfth."

A PHENOMENON OF LIGHT

I saw it from a small plane.
The open socket of the crater
still sputtering
years after the divorce.
The moon-surface of her sides,
the treeless airless feel.
I've seen old photos
of her reflection in Spirit Lake,
snow on the summit like a white veil.
But ah! When she blew
she shipped ashes to Fresno
and filled the lake full of dead trunks
as a toothpick holder on oilcloth.
It must have been too much.
The lonely outpost,
the responsibility of holding down
a corner of Washington,
the lava buildup for years.
Finally mad as a pressure cooker,

she shot trees from her sides,
covering lodges
and campers with her spasms.

I'd come to Oregon with a friend to visit his rela-
tives. His cousin, Hoyt Jarrel, owned a filbert
orchard and a single-engine plane. He wanted to
show us Mount St. Helens with its top blown away.
His dirt runway parted the trees. The house and
machine-sheds were left behind in a clearing like
shipping crates.

We flew north from Portland. I leaned forward
trying to see between the shoulders of the men, but
the seat-belt held me in place and the nose of the
small plane was all I could see. My heart pounded
and I tried to act as if flight were something I did
everyday.

I watched from either side of the plane. Soon we
crossed the Columbia River. Then we were over
Washington. The noise of the engine prevented
conversation with the front-seat passengers. I
gripped the seat and looked across the country. The
swelling hills and trees. The clearings for fields.
Mount Hood, Mount Adams, Mount Rainier, in the
distance. Hoyt knew the terrain. I wished I could
hear everything he said.

It wasn't long until I got a glimpse of Mount St.
Helens over the nose of the plane. I knew it was
Mount St. Helens because the top was flat. I heard

Hoyt say the volcano erupted in 1980. Several times he turned to drive his voice to the back seat. The force of the volcano had blown trees out of the ground, dumped Spirit Lake full of logs. Truman Lodge was under one hundred feet of dried mud. They'd never find it. People had been standing right there looking at the side of the mountain as it swelled several feet a day! They thought something might happen. The last words over one transmitter was that it was finally happening.

Hoyt tilted the wings of the craft so he could see other craft in the area. It also made him easier to see, he shouted to my friend.

The propellers churned with the steady roar of a vacuum cleaner. I wanted to put my fingers in my ears to deaden the noise, but they might see me from the front seat.

I looked from the plane. Now I could see we were almost over the mountain. Six hundred feet of it was gone from the top—Hoyt yelled to us. It was like a huge, primitive bowl with a bite out of the northern side. Inside the crater, I saw the new dome build-up like a wad of mud or clay in the bowl. A small trail of smoke was still rising from it.

The snow that was still on Mount St. Helens in early May looked dirty. The plane circled the crater several times. I noticed the marbled effect of snow on the inner walls of the crater. I felt dizzy from the slant of the plane over the immense opening in the mountain.

I looked at the terrain where lava had spilled—mile after mile. Sometime I saw a patch of green the lava had bypassed. But mostly it looked like we flew over a steep desert, or some aftermath of war. The trees which had not been blown out of the ground during the eruption had been stripped of their limbs and stood like a jumble of telephone poles without wires. The glare off the pale, barren land made me close my eyes.

Hoyt held the small plane steady over the summit. I didn't know if there was wind or not. Hoyt had it together—I knew that from the beginning. He grew filberts, though my friend called them hazelnuts. Shipped them all over the world. He owned a plane, studied instrument flight, could follow what he set out to do. He was practicing his maneuvers the morning the mountain went up with the force of an atomic explosion.

I looked from the plane again as it flew over the crater one last time. I thought of the desolation of the land that would never recover.

There was fog on the ocean as we flew back toward Oregon. I felt covered also, and what I let show was like the desert of Mount St. Helens. I watched my friend sit quietly in front of me. Maybe there was a chance I would want to feel a part of someone again. Maybe someday. Should I tell him later? Would it make any difference if he saw my feelings? Wasn't that the way it was at the end of marriage? When there was talk, it made no difference. Maybe the fragments of my whole life were that ragged crater—that bowl of a mountain broken on one side. Maybe my invisible self—when it was uncovered—was only a hole. Is that why it was so frightening that I gripped the seat until my arms hurt? It wasn't easy to trust a seat several thousand feet in the air with nothing under it. Such desolation. Where had the mountain gone? Strewn for one hundred miles. Dispersed like goods after a marriage. Where was that scene in the picture— Mount St. Helens reflected in Spirit Lake? I had once cut pictures from magazines, hoping even then, I suppose, they'd be tunnels out of my life.

I heard Hoyt say he used a helicopter to blow the filberts off his trees when it was time to harvest. Then he collected the nuts with a sweeping-machine. Hoyt also said he used the helicopter to blow the ashes from Mount St. Helens off the trees. He had even built his own processing plant to dry the nuts after harvest.

I looked down across the land. Everything was green. In places the fields were sectioned like a sheet of stamps. Then I saw the shadow of the plane on the fields below. I looked again because it wasn't a shadow, but a small ball of light. What made it happen? Every time I looked down, I could see the small brightness that followed under the plane. Was it a reflection of the sun through the window of the plane—or off the wing?

My life was different than Hoyt's. But at least my attempts and failures were not the magnitude of the mountain, nor the damage as lasting. No, I decided that I could heal. Even if I felt hollow—maybe it wasn't too late. Maybe it was in these times of seeing something bigger than my own life, that I gained hope. I even liked hearing a man who had come to so much tell how he'd done it.

I saw the tiny ball of light on the ground again as we flew back to Hoyt's landing strip. I liked reminders. They were connections between the duller parts of life when I felt again I was wrapped in a strange glow of light instead of the dark shadows that always seemed to follow.

INITIALLY

Eelibuj had a cat named Roughy whom she called Velcro when she scratched. When Eelibuj moved to another house, Roughy cried in the front seat of the rental truck and moped in the yard. She clawed the flowered sofa when Eelibuj wasn't looking, though sometimes Eelibuj heard her from the other room and yelled. Which upset Roughy Velcro. When Eelibuj went to work cataloging paintings at the museum, she left Roughy alone for the day. In her loneliness Roughy Velcro scratched behind the sofa, but at night she purred in bed with Eelibuj as though she were an oscillating fan on a summer's hot night. And Eelibuj didn't see the scratching until later when she moved the sofa to vacuum, and saw the sofa clawed to the bone. But Roughy didn't budge from her ways. Eelibuj covered the sofa with an old sheet and bought Roughy a scratching-post which sat in a corner of the room. But Eelibuj had faith Roughy Velcro wouldn't scratch the sofa and vowed that a cat should keep her claws. Eelibuj wanted Roughy to prowl in the yard and catch moths and small birds. Once Roughy even brought a young garter snake to the porch. Eelibuj prayed that Roughy would find resolution to scratch in the yard and on her post but not on the sofa. And by faith she renewed her pledge daily. Eelibuj prayed their ways would be prosperous. That the museum would like her cataloging work and that Roughy would hunt in the yard until she was fulfilled. And it was only the next day Roughy caught a bird which she left at the door for Eelibuj. And sat in the wisteria bush glorying. Because we move in his will. Roughy chose to obey the law of Eelibuj and no longer scratched in the flowers of the sofa. Eelibuj removed the sheet that covered her piece of furniture. Yes Roughy took her vow of obedience that day. Though Roughy eating her cat-chow sounded like claws in the sofa, Eelibuj trusted in the Lord. But every voice you hear is not God. No, and Roughy would hear the inner voice again to scratch the sofa. But Roughy Velcro could be strong in the Lord. And in the power of his might. When Roughy was tempted she sat in the corner and looked at her scratching-post. Now Roughy there is power to overcome your shortcomings. Hallelujah. Your anger that you are subject to Eelibuj who pets you, feeds you, and calls you her own. Show me the heart of art. Eelibuj prayed over her job in the museum. She prayed she could resist painting pictures of her own when she was at home by herself in the evening. Wasn't art an outcropping of a willful heart? Wasn't it truly iconic and could not please God? Eelibuj determined only to make lists of the art that already was. And resisted her temptation to create. She would be an example to Roughy. But the urge to claw the sofa returned to Roughy Velcro when Eelibuj was at work. It became truly threadbare, showing its shins to the wall. Eelibuj prayed the sofa would get healed. She prayed the corners would return. The petals of the tapestry. Oh evil art. She prayed in tongues or spoke Roughy Velcro's name in initials. She spoke the inner language. Glossolalia. Or cat-tongues. It was the devil's claw she remembered that clung in the fields. How would RV like one of those stuck on the end of her leg? RV should change her ways, but she sat in the window pulling her claws with her teeth, her cat eyes shifting lazily from E to the flowered s. How could Roughy serve with her eyes and disobey with her feet?

 # FIRESTICKS

"I'll take you back to Guthrie."

"You don't have to, Navorn."

"Don't you want to stay longer?"

"No, my father's better. The woman shouldn't have called me to come this time."

"Maybe he just wanted to see you."

"He lays in bed like a stove-pipe man. We don't have a lot to say. He wants to be buried on Mount Scott."

"I talked to the woman in the living room while you were with your dad. She takes good care of him."

"She probably thinks he has some money."

"You're tough on everyone."

"I told him I couldn't bury him on Mount Scott. It's state property. It's solid granite. He's not dead yet."

"Where's Mount Scott?"

"In the Wichita Mountain range. I showed it to you at the last tollgate."

"Those hills?"

"Mount Scott is the highest. They're mountains in Oklahoma."

"Why does he want to be buried there?"

"I don't know."

"You didn't ask him?"

"What are you doing?"

"We can't leave Frederick without looking at antiques."

"You're stopping at Smith's?"

"Old tools, bottles, jars."

Blacksmith's handmade wagon-wheel measure, iron toys, quilts, paperweights, handkerchiefs, rolling pins, wooden ironing boards, glassware, scales, marbles, accordion, pitchfork, doorknobs, keys, trunks, grater, tea towels, rocking horse, hat pins, teapots, planes, one-man cross-cut saw, ice pick, oil lamp, jugs, license plates, toolbox, checkerboard, butter-churn with wooden paddle, postcards of dancing bears, pulleys.

"Jesus."

Medicine bottles, printer's wood alphabet, coins, a birdlike oilcan that makes a "glurp" when pushed on the bottom, tobacco tin, umbrellas, veils, three-legged chair, milk can, sewing basket, signboards, Indian faces, horse collar, depot office desk, biscuit tin, flour sacks, stamps, pitchers, wire hens, lamps, pocket watches, fox tails, old furs, wire basket, calico cat, pocketbooks, used books, canes, Indian rugs, puppet on a string, trombone, comic books, cups, saucers, cartridge belts, cane chairs, toy fire engine, washboard, fans, hat box, shaving brush, howling dog, Indian-head nickels.

"Jesus."

"Don't you like antique stores?"

"Of course I do. Why the hell wouldn't I like a pile of junk."

"It's more than that. It's the leftover lives of people. Don't you wonder about the boy who pushed the toy fire engine along the floor?"

"Do you?"

"You have no imagination."

Wood ducks, doorstep cow, pewter candlesticks like icicles.

"I liked the guns."

"That's the table I usually don't pay attention to."

"And the hunting knives."

"I always think of my Indian grandmother."

"Stamps like square snowflakes with lace-tatting edges, stained with some grim face. Dancing bears, circus ponies."

"Seventy-five dollars for the church pew. I wouldn't pay that for a church pew. Makes me sleepy just thinking about it."

"Chay mah cay. Now the weeds are ghostly in the headlights of the truck."

"What are those strange words you say?"

"Ho twoddy. The Indian words?"

"Yes."

"Yah hoo wee."

"What do they mean?"

"They're kitsch. The leftover bric-a-brac of language. I don't know, Navorn, what they mean. They're praise to the Great Spirit. Sounds that are nearly words. Gimcrack. Or what remains of words after the language is dead."

"Whew."

"They're stubborn remnants. The antique store of words."

"I could stay at your place since I'm driving you back to Guthrie. I could put my bedroll in your corner. You wouldn't know I was there."

"I would know you were there. I like to be alone. I don't want to cook for anyone. I can read when I eat, think about anything I want. I like to be alone. We're meant to stay in our own categories. We're Post-Tower-of-Babel."

"I don't know what you're talking about. Don't you get lonely?"

"I can hear others moving about in their rooms. It's company for me. I like the way light comes in the window in the morning. I've always been alone. I want it that way. Marriage made me uncomfortable. If I let you stay at my place, you'd creep into my room at night."

"That seems to be more on your mind than it does mine, lady."

"I have a small apartment. It's clean. I don't want you there. I want my things as they are. I was always afraid my father would want to live with me. He was somewhat of a dude, like you. He traveled around, didn't always have a place to stay. It was convenient for him to drop in and have me cook and pick up after him for a while. I don't want anyone."

"You're tough, Turley."

"What did he ever do but cause me grief?"

"Why did you go see him?"

"Because he's sick. And he's my father. I have a few feelings."

"Just a few."

Navorn sat at the table near the front window of the Barbed Wire Diner again.

"I thought you were going to Texas."

"I was and still am."

"What's keeping you?"

"I'm in no hurry."

After he ate, I watched him smoke as I served eggs and hashbrowns and ham to my regulars. I wiped tables and carried more orders and picked up my tips until the Diner was nearly emptied of the breakfast crowd.

"What have you been doing for forty years, Turley?"

"My name is Turle. I've been waitressing."

"It should be that easy for a man to get a job."

"I thought you just wanted to travel around the country."

"That's what I've been doing in Wyoming and Nevada and North and South Dakota."

"You don't want to work?"

"Yes I want to work." Navorn folded the paper. "But there isn't much to do unless you're a broad who can wait tables."

I felt the edge of prairie grass around my knees like heated snow. I was a small child kneeling on the prairie, flames licking my legs with small cows' tongues. The knock at the door continued. His eyes crossed to mine like two sparrows.

"What's the matter, Turle?"

"What are you doing here?"

"I thought I'd drive you to work."

"Is it time? Did I oversleep?"

"No. I'll make the coffee."

"I don't have any. I always drink it at the Diner. I think I was dreaming."

"What did you dream?"

"The alarm is going off now."

"So what was your dream?" He followed me into the bedroom. "Was it the Christmas man again?"

"I don't remember."

"You always remember dreams when you wake while you're still dreaming them."

"Let me see. I think it was a fire. Cows coming out of the fire. Yes, that's it. Before things still seem to hold together. But don't quite yet."

"Why do you always talk this way?"

"What are you doing here? I can't get dressed with you in my room. Wait by the door. I can get to the Diner on my own."

"The place is still closed so I thought I'd come and get the waitress. I don't know where Edward lives. He talks about the garden he's going to plant. Butter beans, black-eyed peas, squash, pumpkin, corn, okra, kohlrabi. I had a small farm in Wisconsin. But you wouldn't like it."

"Why not?"

"They drove the Indians out a long time ago."

"Where did they go?"

"Oklahoma, I think. I don't remember. Before my time. Then they let some of them come back."

"Edward lives in a room above the Diner."

"The moon lights up the fields at night. When I was a boy I was afraid the moon would fall. And I wondered if it did, where it would hit, and if I would be pushed down into the earth underneath it, facing a bright white bulb I could do nothing about."

"You people from Wisconsin are strange."

"Maybe the moon is only a hot-air balloon, and will fall like parachute silk."

"It could even fall the other way, away from the earth, and we would always be in darkness at night."

"Except for the stars."

I heard the bell ring one night after dinner. I took the apron from my waist and went to the front door. Navorn stood grinning beneath the light in the hall.

"I thought I'd stop to see you."

"I thought you'd be leaving town."

"I had planned on it, Turle, but couldn't because of your love notes. Let me come in."

Navorn came in the door and closed it. He took me in his arms and kissed me, a long kiss, and I held tightly to him, his hands on my waist and hips. After such a long time it felt good to have a man against me.

"I think you'll get used to this."

"I haven't done the dishes yet."

"Change your ways, Turle."

"I don't sleep with men. Put me down."

"I'm not asking you to sleep with me. Just get under the covers with me and we'll talk for a while. It's a cold world out there. I need comfort."

"Do you sleep in your truck?"

"Sometimes. Do you get in bed with your shoes on?"

"Navorn, I don't like this."

"Just endure it then."

"You're crowding me."

"This is a small bed."

"There should just be one of us in it."

"Get closer."

Navorn kissed my neck and ear. His hand on my breast, then inside my dress, unbuttoning it, pulling it off my shoulder. "I don't like this." He kissed my breast when he got the dress down far enough. "Don't, I said."

"I'm not listening." He stood up and took his clothes off. I looked at the wall. I was uncomfortable looking at the wall, shivering and afraid of what it would be like. I didn't really want him to do it. He pulled my dress the rest of the way down. I felt naked and cold. He spread my legs with his knees, roughly, and was on me. He kissed me several times and put his finger into me. It wouldn't take him long, but I had not made love for so long it wouldn't make any difference how long he took. My feet were cold and it hurt where he pushed himself into me. I put my arms around his shoulders and felt how much he wanted to do it. The light was on in the hall and I could see the closeness of his face when he finished.

"You're like a story I've listened to in the dark." He didn't make sense. But he wasn't hearing a real story anyway. Only part of a story after the heart is gone. When not much is left. The human heart removed from its beating.

"Did it hurt you, Turle, I'm sorry."

"You have a woman in every town you pass. Why should Guthrie be different?"

"I thought you didn't sleep with men."

"Get off."

"Where are you going?"

"To get you an ashtray."

"I thought you were going to do the dishes."

I put my dress on under the covers and came back into the bedroom and gave him the ashtray, feeling his semen run down my leg. I got a towel from the bathroom to wipe it off. I got back in bed and lay next to him while he smoked. When he finished he said he wanted to do it again. "Turle—" I didn't answer but let him have it again. His momentum grew until I felt him pump the semen into me again. He was quiet then. He kissed my mouth and jaw. He moved from me and I pulled my legs together and felt the wetness of the sheet under me. Navorn fumbled for another cigarette. It burned my nose when he lit it.

"Don't get ashes on the bed."

"Oh hell, Turle, what difference does it make?"

"This is my place and I keep it clean."

"Did you like it?"

"It was easy to do, just uncomfortable a moment and somewhat messy, like spilling soup down my chin."

"I like the difficult ones, not those that hang all over me when I walk into a place. I want the ones who don't come after me. I'll find out how to turn you on."

"If there's another time."

"You'll like it after a while."

"I'd like for you to leave me alone."

"No you don't."

"I like it when a man tells me what I'm feeling. Yes, that's what they do best."

"You're like unwrapping a tight-lidded canning-jar with a seal. One that hasn't been opened in a while. You're hard to pry loose. But what's been stored a long time down there in the cellar is still good."

"Don't touch my crotch like that."

"There was a girl like you once in the pulp mill."

"Pulp?"

"It's where I worked before I farmed in Oconto. All the men wanted her and maybe it was because she wouldn't give in."

"Did she ever?"

"She probably did. After I left. Don't they all?"

"You have a way of getting to my heart, Navorn."

"Then there are the easy ones. Not like you."

I had my hand on his chest. I touched his shoulder and ribs. I put my ear to the voice in his chest. I touched his stomach and felt the hair. I moved slowly to his groin, but came back to his chest with my hand. I leaned up and kissed his mouth. He put out his cigarette.

"You can touch me."

"I don't want to. It would get hard again."

"No it wouldn't. It's too soon. Touch me."

I put my hand to his groin again and felt the part of him that had been hard and pumping just a few minutes ago, now soft and curled in the hair. I rested my hand on it for a moment. I felt him twitch.

"I wanted you since I first saw you."

"In the Diner?"

"Yes."

"I remember. I don't need paint. I'm simple."

"To look at and talk to. Don't you want a man?"

"I just had one."

"Touch me," he said again in a commanding voice and I took him in my hand. "Kiss it."

"No."

He pushed my head down to him. I kissed him where he wanted me to, and sucked him. He flared a moment and moved his hips and groaned, his hand on my shoulders, holding me down to him. I used my tongue and teeth, took my mouth away from him. He pulled me up to him and kissed me. Then he was on me, but it wouldn't go in. I was tight and small again. He moved on me and gave up.

"Turle. Use your fingernails."

I did and it grew firmer.

"Get your legs up. Put them on me. Turle use your fingernails."

I wondered when he was going home. I didn't like him in my apartment anymore. Once was enough but he pushed into me again. I used my fingernails, touched him. I moved my hands along him as he pushed in and out. I hoped he would come quickly but it took a while and he moved and moved on me. I wanted to push him off but he moved with rigid momentum trying to reach another climax. I kissed his ear, put my tongue into his mouth, whatever I thought would make him pump again. I used my fingers between his hips, and when I felt his fingers in mine, I told him to stop. After several more spasms of movement, he reached a climax or gave up. I wasn't sure I felt a twitch or not, and didn't feel his semen fall from me when I stood afterwards.

"You're smoking bothers me."

"A lot of things bother you."

"It's late."

"Go do the dishes. I gave up my room for tonight. I don't have a place to sleep."

"You can't stay here."

"My roommate has some girl with him and he wanted to be alone with her. He couldn't get it on with me sitting there, could he?"

"Sleep in your truck."

"It's too cold, damn it."

"But you're from the north. Oconto, remember? Four-fifths? Little land-allotments like postage stamps."

"Five forties, and I'm going to stay here."

"You're not invited."

"That doesn't make any difference."

"Leave."

"I don't know what's wrong with you, Turle. You're a hard woman sometimes. I'm sorry you can't get it off."

"The way you make love? How could I feel anything? You appear at my door with a cow-pasture grin on your face, poke yourself into me before I know what's happening."

"Get your mouth out of the manure pile."

He got up and took a shower while I washed the dishes.

"What have you got to eat?"

"I don't cook for men, remember? This is my apartment and you're messing it up."

"Take a shower."

"I'll fix you a sandwich if you'll leave me alone."

Navorn ate the sandwich and watched television. I told him I had to go to bed because I got up early to go to the Diner.

"I know, remember?"

"I think the bed is too small for both of us. It's just a single."

He followed me into the bedroom and lay down beside me anyway. He put his arm around me and his breath on my neck bothered me. I nudged him when he started to snore. "I don't think I can sleep with you in the bed."

"Yes, you can. Just think of all the women that would like to have me in bed with them."

"Counting them would probably keep me awake all night." He was snoring again within minutes. "Why don't you go out to the truck and get your sleeping bag and put it in the living room?" He reached for another cigarette and lit it. "I'm used to sleeping by myself. Besides, your smoking hurts my nose."

"Your talking bothers my ears. I need to get sleep too, Turle. I have a job to look for." Navorn turned on the small light by my bed and found the ashtray. He turned to a honkey-tonk station on the radio and took several long puffs off his cigarette. I usually read a few pages from a book and fell asleep quickly. Navorn's foot moved in time to the music. I reached under the bed and got my book. I read until he finished his cigarette and turned to the wall. I shut off the radio and light. I looked at the ceiling and walls. The old, high windows. The chest of drawers and Indian blanket. The oil lamp that had been my mother's. I heard Navorn snore. I heard a car go by the apartment building.

I must have slept a while because I woke suddenly and looked at Navorn. I had dreamed of my grandmother's face again. I saw her on the bed in the room before she died. The hair running back on her head like a gray wing. The cheekbones. The closed eyes. I wonder what she saw inside her head. It was as though we met in the clearing and still had nothing to say.

I touched Navorn and told him to be quiet. He got up angrily and dressed. But then he took his clothes off again.

"I'm not going anywhere in the middle of the night." He lay beside me with one arm behind his head. I was sorry I woke him. Finally he slept again and I stayed awake, not sleeping or dreaming. At 4:30, I got up and dressed for work. Navorn got up too, groggy as I was. He dressed and left the apartment.

The door stood open behind him.

STAMP DANCE

For Jim Moore

Uncle Al teased him. "Here Mack, you want to go somewhere?" He put a canceled postage stamp in his hand.

Mack looked at the small square. "Marianne Moore American Poet 1887–1972 25 USA." He read. "What does she do?" Mack asked.

"Mails things." Uncle Al gave his usual lack of information.

But Mack didn't let Uncle Al go.

"Electric bills. 'Sorry I can't marry you today' letters. 'Buy more magazines and become a millionaire.' " Uncle Al was pleased with himself.

Now Mack acted uninterested.

"You know the mailboxes? The Post Office with the flag where you went with your ma when your daddy was overseas?"

Mack looked at him.

"Where you went for food stamps."

Now Mack knew. But he didn't remember Marianne Moore.

"She might have been there and you never saw her." Uncle Al laughed at himself and Mack wondered what was up.

"Yes, but I couldn't see what my mother did over the counter." Mack said.

Mack held Marianne Moore in his hand. She had a pink face and a rose at her collar. A light shined up in her face. He looked at the dark blue background around her. Royal blue.

But what did Poet have to do with Marianne Moore? He got the post office part. But what did *e* and *t* stand for if she was a mail handler? Why didn't it say Pomh? Marianne had her hand to her cheek.

Uncle Al put another canceled stamp in Mack's hand. It wasn't Marianne Moore at all, but a bird. In fact, it was an eagle.

"Why's an eagle crowded on a stamp?"

"There's lots of things on stamps." Uncle Al poured the last of the milk in a glass for himself. "There's whole stores that sell stamps," Al said. "Nothing but. There's lots of birds and animals. Whole series of them."

"How did you get to one of those stores?" Mack wondered. "And what are they for if you can buy stamps at the post office?"

"Well, there's collectors." Mack's friend, Billy, told him in Mack's attic room. "They keep them in books in drawers. Foreign stamps. Old stamps."

Mack had never heard such things.

"They make special books with plastic pages and you put the stamps in them."

"Why?"

"Just to collect them."

"How do you get them?"

"The same as you get everything. You buy them."

Mack tasted the back of Marianne Moore. Some of the glue was still shiny. It was so the stamp would stick to the letter. Mack held it in his hand. The dirt under his fingernails made thin black curves.

Mack sat in the attic room after Billy left. The oak tree and the street light raked at the window in the eave. Mack had a box under his bed, and a helmet on the wall with a horsehair tail. He didn't know where it came from. Maybe one of Uncle Al's girlfriends.

The back corner of Marianne Moore was still sticky. He stuck it to his bedpost. He wished he had a book to put it in. He wished he had a drawer for the book with the one stamp in it. He kept his socks and underwear in the box under his bed.

When Mack's mother went for money orders to pay the bills, Mack begged to go with her. Mack had hated to go in the past. Before she got a job. When they lived on food stamps. She'd yell at him for wandering away from her in line. She'd yell at him for standing on her shoes. She didn't know why Mack didn't stay with Uncle Al, except Mack always wanted to go places.

"United States Post Office." He read the large letters on the building. He saw the flag. He knew the Post Office was a place connected to the government. He knew it was a place connected to the world. It was even connected to life because the Post-Office man had given his mother the food stamps. And it was connected to war and death because it was where his father had come to sign up for the army. The Post Office was where Mack and his friend, Billy, would register when they turned eighteen.

But Mack's father made it back from Viet Nam. When Uncle Al called him "missing in action," it was the war in the city he meant. In whatever there was that called men away from their families and out into the streets never to come back again. Mack wasn't sure where or why but he heard stories of how his ancestors roamed the prairies following buffalo. Now they couldn't hunt. There was even the notice of the annual Indian shoot that appeared in spear-fishing season.

The stamps were like angels that took things away. But where was Marianne Moore? The large marble corridors echoed with people's coughs and footsteps.

Mack saw the large open-mouthed canvas sacks waiting on racks to be closed and taken to the trucks on the loading dock. He watched the customers buying stamps, mailing packages and letters. In a corner was a "slippery when wet" sign. Two small posts held a rope that looped lazily on the floor. The shiny marble corridor begin to slither with its brown and gray patterns. Mack thought of the snake he'd seen on the science table in school.

The square boxes along the wall were like the apartments where his friend, Billy, lived. They were like Indian cliff-dwellings his teacher showed him in a book. There was mail in some of the boxes. It leaned at the same angle in every box and reminded

Mack of snow on the window of his attic room in the winter.

At school Mack wrote an essay on "My Stamp Collection." He used words like "perforated." His teacher told Mack she'd save her stamps for him and praised his paper.

When he saw stamps on envelopes in the crooked tin wastepaper basket in the office, he wanted to steal them. Even Uncle Al still blessed him with an occasional canceled stamp he tore from an envelope.

But Mack wanted a new stamp. Not one always crossed with bars. He told Uncle Al that he and Billy would go to the store for his lottery ticket if he'd given them a nickle. Uncle Al even gave Mack several pennies for staying out of his room for a while. It made Uncle Al's girlfriend laugh.

Mack told Billy he wanted to go to the Post Office one day after school. "You can come," Mack said as he counted his money.

Billy said he could go, but on the first day Mack planned the trip to the Post Office, Billy came crying to the door of the school. He had lost his glove and would get beat when he got home, he said. His father would be waiting.

They walked back to Billy's locker. They asked in the office. They walked through the halls. Mack told Billy he'd go with him to Billy's father, but Billy wouldn't let him. Mack was afraid to go to Billy's house anyway. They should cover his father with stamps and send him somewhere.

It made cold fish swim up Mack's spine.

"Candied Pike," Uncle Al called that feeling.

Mack started out on his own, but he walked a long time and never found the Post Office. His footsteps on the walk made him think of the fists of Billy's father.

When Mack got home, he asked his mother where the Post Office was, and he had been going in the right direction. He just hadn't gone far enough.

The following week Mack asked Billy again to walk to the Post Office with him, but Billy couldn't. His father would find out about it, and he'd get beat again. Billy couldn't do anything. Mack had seen the cut under the bandaid over his eye.

They should cover Billy's father with stamps and send him somewhere.

It was twelve blocks to the Post Office. Mack counted them this time. They wouldn't miss him at home. They might think he was under the plaid bedspread on his rumpled bed where he slept when he stayed up too late. Or they would think he was hiding out with Billy after his father hit him again. Sometime they could climb through Mack's attic window up the oak tree to the roof and sit against the chimney.

Mack peered into the Post Office. The large corridors. The echo. There was always a line. His heart pounded. Someone behind him opened the door and pushed him in. He walked slowly to the people who stood like they were going to the lunchroom.

"Next," the people behind the counter kept saying in their uniforms. Yes, the Post Office was a very important place. It kept you alive or sent you away. Whatever it chose to do. Mack stood straight in line. He watched people move up to the counter one by one. How restless he had been when he'd come with his mother. How often she had told him to stand still as she waited.

Mack looked at the stamps in the display case. Why hadn't he seen them before? There were birds, dinosaurs, badgers, fish. There were ships, trains. There were even airplanes. Bombers and jets that took people far away. There were famous men, even Indians. Or their war bonnets, at least. There was even, yes, Marianne Moore! Without the bars on her face. Looking at him with her hand to her cheek just like his teacher standing over his desk. Post Office Elementary Teacher. That's what the "Poet" meant on her stamp.

Suddenly the "next" was for him. He didn't know what to do. The woman behind him nudged him forward. "It's your turn." She said.

Mack walked to the counter and looked up to the man. His heart pounded again. "How much are stamps?"

"$12.50 for a sheet of fifty. $25.00 for one hundred."

Mack stood with his mouth open. The man spoke so fast Mack couldn't hold it in his head.

Marianne would be watching with that teacher-look on her face.

The man held up a sheet of stamps. "There are fifty on a sheet for $12.50."

A sheet of stamps? No one told him they came in sheets. What would anyone do with that many stamps? Who had that much money? Mack couldn't think what to do. He held up his hand with the sweaty money. Several nickels and many pennies.

"You want just one stamp?"

Mack nodded his head.

"Any particular kind?"

"No." Mack said.

The man looked through his drawer.

The Indian war bonnet. Mack wanted to say.

"I—" Mack tried to speak and the man looked at him. He thought everyone across the counter and everyone in line behind him was looking. "The headdress—" Mack pointed, and the man handed Mack the feathered war bonnet.

"Next," the man said.

If Mack saved his money forever, he wouldn't be able to buy a sheet of stamps. Why would anyone want that many? How could there be that many people to mail letters to? Mack didn't know anyone to write to.

But maybe he did.

Mack knew he could trust stamps. He would write a letter to his father wherever he was. The stamp would find him. Mack would write to his father to come home even if he beat him. Though he wouldn't. Not Mack's father. Mack would share the attic room with him. The dark plaid bedspread. They could watch their white breath rise together in the winter like the vapor trail of a faraway plane above the dark walls that curved like the dirt under fingernails.

Mack revised his "My Stamp Collection" essay. He would send it to his father too. Now he knew that stamps came in large squares like the map of their state sectioned off in counties the teacher had on the schoolroom wall. She talked to them about geography with her hand to her face. The sheets could be pulled apart like Mack's family had been. Billy said it was better that Mack didn't have a father.

That night Mack drifted off into sleep thinking of the stamps he had collected on his bedpost. In a dream the stamps were wings of white, creamy birds. They blew off the bed in flocks like geese he'd seen lift from a lake. Then they changed their flight and came back. They landed and lifted again and their movement over the water was a stamp dance. Everything was shimmering. Even Billy waved to him with dinosaur stamps on his face instead of the school-nurse's bandaids.

Yes, Mack had to show Billy the Post Office. They could go on long migrations setting out across the world. In one of those open-mouthed sacks they could go anywhere.

THE ALLIGATOR KING

Ajax drove her Cadillac down Mount Rainier Road. The Jesus bumper-sticker splashed through the ruts.

Mott heard the car nose into the landing field of the yard. She looked up from her chair on the porch. If only the Cadillac had wings it would be a helicopter. Or a whirling angel. If only Mott could see things like Ajax did. But Mott thought the Cadillac looked like an alligator in the drive, eye-level in the swamp.

Ajax had just heard that Mott's husband left her for a woman even older than Mott. Ajax also heard that Mott's house was broken into. She lost pew-terware that had been her great-grandmother's, her new television, pie-wheels, her grandfather's sheep castrater. His fleem and hocking knives. And of course Ajax knew Mott faced surgery. Not the cosmetic kind that would help her look good as the older woman who had run off with Mott's husband. No, hers was ordinary. And Mott didn't have insurance. Ajax also had a friend who worked in the bank. She knew Mott's account was overdrawn. And Ajax heard that Mott's son enlisted the night before the morning news was full of a military crisis in a country where he was headed.

Sometimes things seemed to happen all at once. But Ajax was rushing to tell Mott that Jesus was the blessed hope. We were armored in him. When we had faith we wore heavenly scales of metal. We were never given more trials than we could handle. Yes, Mott must be a strong woman.

Mott sat with her elbow on the table. A fly hissing at her face. Her flash cat with the jelly-roll tail curled at her ankles, either sleeping as if dead, or racing back and forth in the yard.

There was, yes, this life full of trials. Ajax told Mott. But we are rewarded in the end. Just look at Ajax and remember how things blow past. Ajax's own son-in-law had been flying over Mount St. Helens in his small plane when it went spurting and erupting and belching and spewing all over Washington and Oregon, and, yes, he had come back. Why, her own grandmother had been nearly killed in a landslide and she survived.

Ajax was in the end-of-time mood and Mott knew she'd have to ride it out. Mott could never get in the Jesus frame-of-mind. She sat on the porch listening hollowly to Ajax. How soon life was over, Mott thought. Her family gone, the world in turmoil, old age squirting in her face. Where had it gone? The blessedness whizzed by so quick she hadn't known it.

"Well, it's cherry pie on a flowered oilcloth when we're in the Lord's hands," Ajax said.

Mott stared at the taxidermied Cadillac and the postage-stamp print blouse Ajax wore. She looked at the little scalloped edges of the stamps. They had the power to transport, like faith. Yes, Ajax had the stamp king written all over her. The alligator king parked in the drive. An earthly shadow of a spirit-mode of travel.

"I remember the house we had when I was growing up in Portland," Ajax said. "I slept sometimes on the screened porch when my father and mother banged their heads together inside. I decided then under the black wool sky packed with sparkling mothballs of stars, I was not alone. No sir. There was someone out there with me. Christ, the Lord, if no one else."

"Life is a fucker," Mott said. "Constantly turning up with a pop quiz we aren't prepared for." Volcano. Earthquake. Tornado. War. Famine. Pestilence. Taxes. Poverty. Loss. Loneliness. Tooth decay. Drought. Flood. Death.

Ajax put her hand on Mott. "Jesus, look down on our faith," Ajax swore, her voice rising from the damp porch. "Overlook our sins."

But how could Mott trust Ajax? Driving a fourteen-year-old Cadillac was like believing a whale swallowed Jonah. Ajax felt guilty that disaster never struck her. She had to think up a reason. Ajax was a crusader while Mott sat on her porch and received what came. Were some people just like that? Ordained to believe or not to believe from the beginning. Maybe faith was the answer. If she could get her mind onto a postage stamp.

Yo. In the meantime, this life was a whammo, Mott thought, hitting us without asking. Its dumb whining in our ears, its ass all askew. The Cadillac like an alligator sinking into the grin of its grillwork, the headlights of its half-opened eyes.

Ajax had always annoyed Mott. In school she had made little smile-faces over her name. In fact, she still did. Ajax had worn a rickracked squaw-shirt and starched crinolines. In her stamp-blouse, she remained glitzy as a tourist trunk pasted with foreign stickers, though Ajax had never been anywhere. Yet Mott tolerated her. Their mothers had been friends. Their fathers were second-cousins.

When Ajax spurted on the porch, Mott could almost see down that long corridor of faith. Yes, life was something shoved down our throat, up our knees, had its tongue in our mouth before we knew it. But we weren't licked. No, Jesus. We were armored. We could throw open our arms. Our legs. We could open wide our teeth and say, Hallelujah. Hallelujah.

FIRESTICKS

I waited for a phone call about my father. The woman who cared for him said that she would call before I went to work. But it was time for me to leave and she hadn't called.

I stood at the window thinking I should put on my uniform. Why didn't Navorn call? I knew he was still in town. It was my fault. I had driven him away. I picked at the flannel robe printed with small cherries.

I could see the snowy fields beyond Guthrie. Brittle clumps of tall grasses stuck through the crust. Clouds rolled in from the North like a herd of wild horses not stopping to graze. Wind bucked the large windows in the rooms I had above a storefront. I looked across the street. Rows of red brick buildings hunched around an early sun. The buildings of Guthrie were turn of the century, some restored, some boarded and vacant. The brick and red-stone buildings the same as the red soil that stained the snow, and had stained my shoes and clothes. How many years had I seen that red soil splattered on cars that came from country roads to Guthrie? That same town where almost a month ago, a drifter came in off the highway in his truck and stopped at the Diner where I worked. The next day he took me to see my father in Frederick, almost two hundred miles away. Then he changed his mind, did not go to Texas where he was headed, but brought me back to Guthrie. But he irritated me with his presence and I told him I didn't want to see him again. Now I faced the emptiness without him.

Was it worse than the emptiness with someone? Did anything last? I'd seen it a thousand times. All in Guthrie. A man would pick up a waitress and it would be fine for a while. Then she'd be alone again, crying, I told myself. Or if the relationship with Navorn did last, I would be stuck with someone I didn't want to be with.

I put on my uniform and got my coat. It was after 6:00 A.M. Usually I was at the Diner by then, but I waited for the call. My footsteps crunched like an old man eating toast in the Diner. Rust-red water ran from under one slab and took my shoe in its mouth. I had to walk several blocks. The wind was sharp. The sun barely up.

"Damn soil comes up from underneath and stains everything." I muttered, but the breath hurt in my throat, and I closed my mouth. I remembered my mother angry about the stains on my socks and clothes when I got home from school. The soil was like the Indian skin that came up from below the surface of my dreams and reached into my thoughts. It was like the face of my ancestors that haunted me when I looked at my dying father.

I could call Navorn. I would need to get to Frederick anyway. I should already be on my way. My father was dying. The woman that cared for him had been up for three nights. He couldn't last many more. But I hesitated. He'd always left my mother and me. Nothing permanent in this life. I didn't want to be with him. What did we have to say? I was better off in Guthrie working. Then I could at least help with his keep. I didn't want to stand beside his bed. I talked about the Diner, about Guthrie, the few people we knew.

"What's the temperature?" I asked, rushing into the Diner. "I didn't listen to the radio this morning."

Edward looked at me. "It's about twenty-six." He paused. "You had a call from Frederick."

"When?"

"About 5:30 this morning. Your father passed away in his sleep."

I called the woman who had cared for him. She'd been up with him most of the night, as she had the past several nights. He dozed off finally about 4:30, and when she looked in on him about 5:00, she couldn't hear his breath. She called the doctor. He pronounced my father dead. She called the Diner thinking I would be there. I would try to get to Frederick by afternoon.

The phone rang at the place Navorn was staying a long time.

"Hello."

"It's Turle Heppner. I need to borrow your truck."

"I don't loan my animal to anyone."

"I have to go to Frederick. My father died this morning."

"What time is it?"

"6:20. I've called my father's sister in southern Oklahoma. I've had a cup of coffee. Now I need to go to Frederick. Did I wake you?"

"Of course, lady, you did."

"Come to the Diner and I'll give you something to eat."

"No, Turle. You only call when you want something."

"You only come over because you need a place to stay."

"I can't today. I'm looking for work. Or I might move on. Something's got to happen."

"Navorn. I have to get to Frederick."

"Take the bus."

"The bus doesn't leave for a while and it takes too long. I need to go now."

"Sorry, Turle."

"You've never lost a parent. You don't know how it feels. Now I have no one. Both my parents are dead."

"Borrow Edward's car."

"I can't blame you for not wanting to take me to Frederick. It's damned cold out there. But I have to make funeral arrangements. I should have done it before this. If I could get down there, I would have it done by this evening. I could receive people tomorrow and he would be buried the next. I'd be back to work in three days."

My father was dead. I took those words through my mind again and again. My father had been a stranger to me. He was a ghost, and he had died. For many years, I had gone on living as though he was already dead. I remembered the times he was supposed to call on my birthday and I never heard.

I shuffled my hands together. Maybe Navorn was right. I was insensitive. Maybe he would be hungry. We had had fun. I acted as though I ignored him. He acted like the irate customer, impatient for his meal. We had gotten along, then he stayed the night and I could not sleep with him in my small bed. I had come to the Diner the next morning with sleep pushing into my head like an animal that came around the trash cans behind the Diner.

Why had I been impatient with him? Why wasn't there room in my life for someone? He called me a man-hater, but I didn't hate Navorn. But neither could I make room for him in the place I rented above the storefront. That was mine. I felt anger that any man would want to move in.

I called the bus station but I already knew the schedule. I wouldn't get to Frederick until late at night.

I called Navorn again. It didn't take long for him to answer.

"Navorn, I want you to think about taking me to Frederick."

"I've just been thinking about it, Turle, and I decided it isn't for me."

"Have you looked outside?"

"I've hardly been out of bed."

"Clouds are coming in from the North. I'm afraid of snow. I could borrow Edward's car. I've got a friend, Kay Fosher, and I could borrow hers. But I don't want to drive alone. Remember how I go to sleep?"

"I told you to take the bus. You've got all day."

"I have to make funeral arrangements."

"They'll wait for you."

"I'll pay you."

"No."

"Don't be a sorehead. Just because we didn't get along when you were at my place."

"You've got a tight world for yourself, Turle. There's no room for any man."

"I'll pay your gas and meals."

"I thought you didn't like a man who sponged off a woman."

"It would get you almost to the Texas border."

"You've got a good memory, lady."

"Don't give me a hard time, Navorn. Get your ass over here. I need you for a few days."

"Is it always what you want? Have you ever thought what I need? What's the weather today?"

"I've already told you. I listened to the radio and there might be a storm. There's a lot of noise in the Diner now, and I can't always listen. Storms come up quickly on the prairie. I can see the clouds from the cafe window crossing the horizon like a turtle. But maybe it's too cold to storm after all."

"Maybe we should both stay in Guthrie."

"I can't. My father died. I've got to go to Frederick."

"All right, Turle, but this is it. I'll get you down there and back and then we're through. You'll have to help with gas."

"That's fine. I won't need to go to Frederick anymore after this."

Navorn wore a hand-knit sweater when he came in the Diner.

"What woman spent her life making that for you?"

"My mother."

"I like it." I smiled. I had only seen his worn belongings in his truck: blanket, bedroll, ripped backpack, nothing with a life or style of its own that anyone would want. He could leave them anywhere and they'd be there when he returned.

We stopped at my place for me to change clothes. There was a pear in the window. I took it with me.

We passed the familiar stores: Jelsma Abstract, the Gaffney Building, Caddo Variety, Guthrie Antique and Monument. The Waterworks. Snake Creek and then the highway south. At least, I wouldn't have to face my dead father and the ancestors that hovered near him by myself.

The wind shoved Navorn's truck. Longspurs made their swift, erratic flight over the highway and across white fields. I watched the muddy snow at the edge of the road as we drifted over the slight roll of the prairie.

Navorn smoked for a while. "That rounded hill with a tuft of brush on it reminds me of the helmet I made once in school. A damned German papier-mâché helmet. The things that come to one's mind."

"I've had strange thoughts too since my father has been sick. I've dreamed of buffalo herds and

Indians. I could almost smell the council fires. Maybe the ancestors can't go to the hunting grounds until they pass their baggage on to some progeny, until they can shake off earthly concerns like lint from their deerskin leggins and breechcloth. It must have passed from my great-grandfather through my grandmother to my father and now me." I still held the pear in my hand.

"And where will it go from there? Where will you leave your legends so you can go to the hunting grounds?"

"I don't have any legends to pass on. I'm satisfied to work in the Diner and spend my evenings at my place above the storefront."

"We should all have a legacy to leave. That's one of the reasons I started out from Wisconsin."

"My father's sister has children and grandchildren. Maybe it will pass to them. I'm removed from that culture. I hardly know it."

"But you're Indian in your ways."

"What do you know of Indians?"

"Nothing, really. Other than the pow-wow I stopped at in the Black Hills. But if I did, you'd be like what I know."

"Why did you change your mind?"

"To take you to Frederick?"

"Yes." I turned the pear in my hand.

"You wouldn't get off my ass."

"But why, other than that? I don't even want to go. I'm afraid of the dreams I have. I don't like Indian ghosts. I don't like to see dead people." I ate the pear with my wool gloves on. The juice ran from my mouth. "Do you want a bite?"

"No."

"It tastes like wool mittens and mothballs anyway. I saw it on the windowsill and brought it with me. Bite?" I asked again, and held it to his mouth.

He backed away. Presently, he lit a cigarette. We rode in silence for a while. I threw my pear out the window. The weather had grown warmer.

When we got to Frederick, my father already had been taken from the house of the woman who cared for him. I talked to a minister, who was there waiting for me at her house. What Scripture should he use? What music? Did my father have a plot? No. I had to pick one. Did I know a funeral cost several thousand dollars? Did my father have money? No. Did I? No. Cremation or a county burial? Had he lived there long enough? It didn't matter for an indigent. He had a sister. And me, with a small savings. Did we want the state to bury him as a pauper?

"Bury him and I'll pay. It will take a while. My father wanted to be buried on Mount Scott. Can you imagine?"

Navorn, in the corner looking at me, motioned for me to come when the minister left. He took me in his arms and held me for a moment.

We had an early dinner with the woman where my father had stayed, and prepared to go to bed after we talked for a while. We would attend a private service for my father in the morning, and then return to Guthrie. His sister decided not to come because of the weather. I would sleep in my father's room. Navorn would sleep on the couch in the living room.

"Isn't there any other place?" I asked.

"The only other room is mine," she said.

"Don't be spooked. I changed the sheets."

Navorn said that he could think of another place. If I needed him I could call. But I ignored him.

"It hasn't snowed in Frederick like it did farther north in Oklahoma." The woman watched the news. "But I think it's going to rain."

When we said good night, she gave me a silver belt-buckle and a pipe which had been my father's. I closed the door to the dark, mahogany room where my father had died not sixteen hours ago. I shivered. The thought that he was dead still jarred me. I sat on the bed for a while. I wondered what the next day would bring. Navorn would be with me, and the woman who took care of my father. I wouldn't be alone with him.

I must have fallen asleep quickly because I woke with a start and the light was still on. I had heard something. Trash cans knocked over? No. I was in Frederick and not at the Diner.

"Navorn," I called, but there was no answer.

I sat on the bed a while longer until weariness overcame me again. I turned off the light. I must have fallen asleep quickly. I dreamed of a wild herd of horses that rattled the windows. I sat up quickly. Lightning flashed. It was thunder I heard.

"Navorn," I said louder, but there was still no answer.

I laid back on the pillow and pulled the covers to my chin. It was just a winter rainstorm. It was just thunder. I had heard it before.

I dreamed again of wild horses and a herd of buffalo. One Indian wore a German helmet made of papier-mâché. Then I lost sight of the road just a moment when we passed a truck and it splashed the windshield with rain from the road. Navorn! He turned on the wipers. Arrows flew. Mud streaked the road. Soil like the mahogany room in which I woke, slept.

What did they have to say to me? The warm breath of the horses steamed the plains. Long grasses moved beside the road. I saw antelope running and I saw buffalo, herds and herds of buffalo, as they once had been on the prairie. I took my hand from the covers and touched them, their rank, brown bodies, their large heads and small eyes. They spoke to me. It once had been their range and I saw the animals: wolves and bears, Indian tribes making camp, thriving on the land. Just as someone someday might get a vision of what our lives had been. They came back not to haunt nor accuse but to remind that they once had been, and still moved with the swirling wind on the plains and the clouds across the sky. I saw herds of wild horses and turtles crawl with the movement of the earth. Great Spirit of the Indian tribes and buffalo. Great Spirit of the Earth.

AN AMERICAN
PROVERB

We live with acts of God. But God isn't in it like
us. Not in any way. He's the one who owns the
land allotments, the words. He sends the little
people to mess up our lives.

What do we know? Born into this world.
Driven up the hill to school. Licked like postage
stamps.

If we look at the blue sky's curtain hiding us
from the hunting grounds, we can't know it yet or
who would be left to stay?

Sometimes I think I should still be writing him.

Now I have to get up in the night and go into
the little rollaway on the back porch. Even in winter,
I sleep there. Once he woke almost glowing. The
field he said the field. Helicopters flying and men
screaming. The guns. Viet Cong running over

them, men gurgling in their own blood, arms and hands and legs shot off not yet dead and he saw by god the acts of God. He saw the angels sweating. They wore headbands and guns on their backs between their wings. They rode horses with braided tails and war masks. They lifted the dying onto their horses and rode off. Up past old cattle trails, the buffalo herds stampeding like comets.

When you're so far away you don't know what's going on anymore. That's the way I like it. It's why I stay here. The only other place I'd like to go is space. Up there in the hereafter. I don't think much of the little blue speck down there in the bottom of the well like a stone. Turning in the waters as if it were something.

Ha.

It's time to do things in a different way. Tear up old standards. Barriers.

We're not supposed to do what it seems like we should be doing. But follow sometimes the trail even when it seems not right. Flying a helicopter by instrument flight. You have to fight against your instincts. You think you're going straight and you're traveling in circles.

"Will you get off the paper when I'm trying to read it?"
"What do you want?"
"A Sunday morning without the dizzies. The bomb drop."

He meck ta.

Sometimes he wanders blind in space. I see his
eyes smell the campfire and I know he's nearing
home. I feel it with my heart.

No they can't push us around. We stand our
ground. We're the watchdog of the world. The
sayers of the way life is.

POLAR BREATH

Now she was an old woman with a cat, who had spent her life raising children and living with a man she didn't love. She hadn't been anywhere but on her own place. She was an exile in herself. For her, pleasure was her house in its cluttered order with all the rowdiness out.

She leased her field and makeshift barn. She didn't even have to feed the animals anymore. She could be at peace, but the spirits wouldn't let her. They stayed in the woods during the day. They camped outside her house at night.

She would spend the afternoon ironing, remaking a dress to wear another year. All she asked was to have the day to herself while her cat slept on the papers and scraps of material in the brown chair by the east window.

From the kitchen window, she watched a red squirrel dig in the hard ground. Once in a while it stood on its hind legs to make sure no one came.

Then it rooted again. Finally it found the nut and sat chewing.

She saw the old tree wrapped in its gross bark, its eyes where branches had been. Across the field, traffic moved on the highway. She could hear the trucks at night. From the upstairs window she could even see their lights pass like a shooting-gallery across the field. They stirred no desire in her to travel.

Beyond the kitchen window there was the bush, the garden and grape arbor, the white fields and a neighbor's barn. Beyond that, a church with its steeple. Then sky above it, without its lack of conformity, pale as the ground.

She watched the squirrel again. Chewing with quick bites, then running up the tree. What bothered squirrels? She saw one sometimes on the road, run over by a car. But that was all. Maybe cars were their natural predator. Tan Buicks.

She nibbled a cracker at the sink. The squirrel was back again. The wind blew backward against its fur. Its tail bushed out like a cape. She pushed some kettles and jars out of her way. On the floor, a pail of water seemed to have a thin film of ice.

The week before, she had driven her old car out of the shed and gone to the grocer in town. She could last a long time without getting out again. It seemed the old furnace ran constantly now, if she'd let it. The thermometer outside fell below zero. The spirits wouldn't stay in the woods anymore. They'd come and sit around her flue and chimney.

Now three blue jays sat in the bush. She wondered if the spirits were near, but she didn't see them. Farther away, there was only the tree looking at her. She finished the crumbs of her cornbread at the sink, and stuck the image of the birds on the walls of her head. She would keep the world as it should be. Even if the spirits ran around her house in the freezing gusts of wind.

She had pictures of her children on a table by the window where the cat slept. Her son and two daughters. She even had a picture of her husband though she'd seen enough of him. He sat there in his green-and-orange plaid shirt, with his bear-claw and his black hair slicked back. He smiled like he was still sitting in his icehouse on the lake. She had taken his stamp collection and pasted some of the stamps on the frame. She'd papered the cellar shelves with the rest. Her son was mad at her for it, but now she could do what she liked.

Once in a while she still woke in the mornings with the stale thought of him on her mind. He must have sneaked around inside her during the night, climbing the mattress coils of her brain.

Out the back window she saw her barn, leaning slightly toward the south, still mostly white, but the red underneath was bleeding through. In another summer or two, the barn would be rust.

She thought of the black-and-white check dress she worked on. It was probably ten years old and she wanted to change the sleeves. The flannel had worn thin at her neck. She would turn the collar around and it would be a new dress. Maybe she'd tighten the waist and sew on new buttons. Yes, that's what she'd do. It would take several days.

She looked through the patches of frost on the kitchen window and saw that the bird-feeder was empty. Why hadn't she noticed? Maybe that's what the blue jays had been waiting for, their blue tails striped with black like tire-marks on a small, plowed field.

She went to the cellar for birdseed and she also got a jar of her pickles. She liked the close-darkness of the cellar under the kitchen. Sometimes she didn't even turn on the light because she knew where everything was.

Back in the kitchen she got her coat and galoshes. She put a scarf around her head and found her gloves. Her cat came into the kitchen to go with her. He wouldn't go out anymore by himself. Other cats bothered him and he was too old to fight. He let them have their way in his territory, even when she shamed him.

The two of them found their way through the clutter in the kitchen. She unbolted the door and they walked through the snowy yard to the bush at the west of the house. She poured birdseed into the feeder. What were those funny tracks? Her cat stayed by the tree smelling them. Ah! She knew. The spirits in raccoon-feet to camouflage their sneaking around her house. Could it really be them? Were they already brave enough to come to her house in daylight?

Inside again, she noticed the feeder was crooked. Would the birds fall off while they tried to eat? She got a string and some old scissors from the drawers. Maybe the bush had shifted with snow, or grown one-sided over the summer. She clipped the shorter string and tied the feeder to the branch with a longer string.

The birds chattered in the fir trees by the front corner of the house, dusting the yard with more snow. Maybe they made all that noise to comfort one another in the cold. She wished she could gather them all into her house. Why didn't their little bodies freeze like ice-cubes? What kept them warm? Their little hearts beating fiercely like an old coal stove? How many shovels had she shucked into one of them?

She saw her neighbor pouring a bucket on his garden rows. Probably sheep manure. He was far away but he waved at her and the howl of his black dog broke the cold. Her cat looked up, alarmed.

On the edge of her garden she found a cob emptied of its corn. It sparkled on one end with frost. She looked at the muffin-tin shape. The honeycomb openings where the kernels had gone. She decided the spirits left it there. Everytime she moved they snipped another detail from the world. They had taken enough from her. Now she was getting parts of it back, sucking them deep within herself. She felt her bowels rumble. The thick branches of the bush stitched a net for her. The empty garden rows. All of them growing like frozen vines around her. Maybe she'd disappear into them someday.

Inside the house once more, she wiped a place to look through the window. Her cat would be scratching at the door soon. She lit the stove and boiled water for tea. She saw that the wet teabag looked like birdseed. She turned the furnace down even farther when it came on. She didn't want to call the gas truck yet. She would wear her coat and scarf, her galoshes and gloves in the house.

Where was her needle? She needed to work her fingers. They felt blue and cold. She'd sew a bright pocket on the dress she was working on. A pocket to help her remember everything she saw. Things she noticed, thoughts she wanted to store in her head. The bush with the blue gas-flame of the blue jay's heads. The pattern of frost growing on the windows. How it covered the glass like ancient cave markings or the scribblings of a child. No, it wasn't the frost at all. It was the spirits that got loose when it was cold. The north wind opened up a highway and they slipped right down to the Great Lakes from the north. Hadn't she seen them after her husband died last winter? Hadn't she heard his ice-fishing decoys rattle one night? Weren't the spirits a pale blue when she looked from the window, floating around the house like manta rays? Their graceful edges undulating in the dim light from the window. Now they were wrapping her house in cellophane. She knew it as she stood at the sink looking out. Something scratched the door and it startled her, but she remembered it was the cat and she let him in.

She knew another secret. They had been in her house. They could walk across the floor without creaking. They could sit on her roof and she'd never know it. Stingrays with their blue-finger edges. Devilfish! She whacked the counter with her broom. The cat ran.

They were coming to take her too. She panicked at the sink. She saw her husband in his icehouse fishing in winter. She felt like she was walking barefoot across the ice to him. She fought to hold to the counter. But she was shuffling across the lake. The drift of cold fog across the ice was like a line of old people. Inside her head, birds flew from the wall. They banged at the windows to get out. Up the road, the church steeple hung like a telephone pole pulled crooked by its wires after an ice storm. How long had she been there? The room circled like the round hole in the ice. She felt the tight hole around her chest. There was something hurting her ankles. She was tangled in the fishing line that went down into the cold, dark hole below her. Now the sun shined its wicked and beautiful pattern on the kitchen window. The cold fog still shuffled across the lake. Something knocked the old cans and kettles from the counter to the floor. She was walking up the road now. Wasn't the afternoon light through the window-frost like a church? How many years had she sung hymns up the road? The little tendrils of the ice like petroglyphs? She heard her children drawing in the frost on the windows. She reached for the finger she saw at the glass. But the ice-hole burped like her old husband in his chair and the frigid water closed her up.

FIRESTICKS

Navorn left Guthrie after my father's funeral. I called him one morning from the Diner. The man whose room he shared said he'd gone to Oklahoma City. I took a package of tablecloths from the storage room and unfolded them over the tables with a whack.

"Sounds like a cattle-drive in here." Edward came from the pantry.

"I'm going down the street before lunch," I said.

"Stop by the bank for me."

"Sure."

I had a friend, Kay Fosher, who worked in the Gaffney Building down the street. "Navorn's gone," I told her. "I called."

"You worry over nothing."

"He might be looking for a job."

"He might be gone to Texas."

I looked at her.

"I thought I'd do some of your worrying for you so you don't have so much."

I didn't say anything.

"You only wanted him to stay when you needed him."

"You sound like Navorn."

"I'm only repeating what I heard you say."

"You should know better than to pay attention to what I say."

"Let's go to the show tonight."

"I don't know if I feel like it. I have some washing I was going to do."

"Do it tomorrow, for heaven's sake."

"I've got to get back to the Diner."

When I returned from the show that night, Navorn was sitting against the door of my apartment.

He touched the brim of his hat like a cowboy. "I heard you coming."

"I always trip over the loose footing on the bottom stair. I thought you'd gone."

He stood and looked at me, a little quieter than usual.

"What's the matter?"

He kissed me in the hall.

"Can't you wait until I open the door?"

He kissed me again when we were inside, then blew his nose.

"I suppose your friend has someone in tonight?"

"No. I have no excuse." He put his head against my shoulder and held tightly to me. "I missed you, Turle. I wanted to feel you against me.

You are the only sane thing I know right now."

I held to him also, feeling the relief of him in my arms.

"The bed is too small for us."

"I'll make one for us on the floor. I know you have to sleep. I've watched you hustle at the Diner, Turle. I don't want to keep you awake."

"I suppose you're hungry too."

"No. I ate in the city."

"Did you find a job?"

"No."

"How long can you go?"

"Some time. I don't have many needs."

"Rent. Food. Gasoline for your animal."

"I feel so left out without money. I feel—" He coughed.

"Are you sick?"

"No."

He had me in his arms and I felt the presence of him in my place. He pulled me to the floor.

"Not on my Indian rug. It's the only thing of value I've got, other than some old Indian baskets."

I washed in the bathroom and put on my robe. Navorn had made a pallet for us on the floor with some sheets and blankets he found in the closet. He pulled me down on him, kissed me and loved as he had before.

Afterwards, I laid beside him on the floor. He had his leg over me and his hand inside my robe on my breast. I felt his breath deepen.

"You've had a long day."

He hardly answered.

"Your leg and hand are heavy."

He moved them.

"No I like your hand on me. Put it back."

I felt his warm hand on my breast again.

"You're a sound sleeper. In Frederick, you said I could call you in the night. I did. Twice. And you didn't answer."

He pretended to hit his head with his hand.

I felt his tired body beside me. I wanted to be closer to him. I wanted to wake him and feel his hands moving on me again, intruding into my body. But he was tired and wanted to fall asleep. His breath on my neck and ear kept me awake again. I went to the bathroom once and slept after I returned. Navorn woke once in the night and reached for a pipe beside his shirt, but he put it down and went back to sleep.

About 6:00 A.M., the alarm went off. He tried to keep me beside him, but I got up and turned it off.

He wanted to make love to me again, but I had to get up.

"Turle." His head was stopped up.

"I have to work." He went to shower.

"Come to the Diner if you want breakfast," I said as I got dressed.

"What if I want you?"

"That's where I'll be too."

"Hell." He pulled the covers over his head.

"Why a pipe?" I saw it on the floor.

"Smoke bothers you, don't it, lady?"

"Yes."

"The pipe?"

"No. I like the smell of a pipe. My father smoked one sometimes."

"I like the smell of you." He kissed me. He had gotten up to blow his nose. He touched me again.

"Lock the door when you leave."

"Don't trip on the stair again."

I had a sore throat after sleeping on the floor with Navorn. I guess it was the draft, or else I caught his cold. I went to the doctor up the street because Edward wouldn't let us work in the Diner if we were sick. I had known the old doctor since we first came to Guthrie. There was a younger one in town, but I liked the old Doc.

I also had an infection the following week, which I finally went to see him about. I suppose it was because I wasn't used to sleeping with a man. My body objected at first to the intrusion of another, but my aches and infections cleared up.

"I'm going to keep fucking you."

"Then help me pay the doctor's bill."

"Navorn, damn it. Is that all that's on your mind?"

He pulled me down to him. "When you're around me, it is." He kissed me and started to unbutton my dress.

"Don't." I wrestled with him. "I have a headache."

He laughed.

"No, I really do. I think it's sinus or else the damned stopped-up nose I caught from you."

"What's the matter with you, Turle?"

"I don't know. I wish you'd leave me alone. I don't want you touching me."

"Yes, I want to." He rubbed my breasts and stomach.

"No." I moaned as he touched me.

He was on me then, fully clothed. I felt his hard body, the friction as he moved himself against me.

"I'm going to wait for you to feel it too," he kissed my mouth and breast when he took off my dress and underwear. He moved his finger in and out of me as though it were bobbing for apples.

"I don't like it when you get me down."

"Yes, you do. Let go of yourself, Turle, and you'll like it even more. Feel how tight you are. Your arms and hips. No wonder your head hurts. Let me touch you. Feel what I'm doing to you."

"No," I shook my head as he put his tongue in my mouth.

He continued to caress me. "What do you think about when I touch you?"

"I think that I would like for you to leave me alone."

He sucked my tongue and breast and rubbed his finger on me. "That's not what you're really thinking. Your body is telling me something different. Hear it?" The sound of his finger moving into me was something like soft rain falling into a barrel.

I opened my legs farther and he pushed his finger into me again. This time I let him.

"I won't hurt you, Turle. Doesn't it feel good?"

"Yes." I pulled my legs together.

"No. Let me do it. Don't hold back from me." He pulled my legs apart again. It was beginning to feel good.

I moaned when he touched me. I longed for him to keep touching me, to keep pushing his finger into me.

He got on me again. "Your headache?" He asked with his mouth pushed against my ear.

"I still feel it a little."

He kissed me, squashed himself against me with his rapid movement. He still hadn't taken off his clothes.

"Maybe I should stop." He got off me.

"No," I said. He kissed and continued the movement of his fingers into me, now two fingers moving with the roll of my hips.

"What do you think about when I touch you?"

"I hear a car starting outside on the street."

"Don't think about that."

"I hear the way the wind sounds over the building."

"Forget what's outside. Think about my fingers. What am I doing to you, Turle?"

"Moving your fingers like the wind over the building."

"Wanting it to come inside."

"Yes, Navorn. Yes." I moved with him.

"What do you feel?"

"I'm thinking about polished apples."

"Turle," he laughed and kissed me.

"I can see the edge of my wine-red shawl on the table. I want you, Navorn."

"Look at me. You always look away from me. Feel my fingers coming into you."

"I feel them."

He continued to fondle me, not breaking his rhythm. "What are you thinking about?"

"When you pull them out, I want you to put them back in. Navorn, I want you."

"Not enough yet."

"I want you."

"Just wait."

"No. I want you now."

"Let go of yourself."

I moaned.

He moved his fingers steadily into me, touching the clit when he brought them out, pushing them in again. Now. Now. In me. His fingers felt like the edge of wind over the building, caressing it, finding a crevice to enter. His fingers felt like the wine-red fringe of my Indian shawl. I heard the moans of my voice pleading for him. I moved my hips, sucked him into me.

He put his mouth on the nipple of my breast. I let go and opened to him. He moved his tongue and mouth over me and I fluttered for him like the round, polished apples in a barrel of water after he finally got one in his mouth.

I heard Navorn on the stairs the next evening. Before I got to the door I unbuttoned my shirt and unzipped my skirt. When I opened the door for him I had one shoe off.

"What are you doing?" He asked.

"Isn't it what you came for?"

"Not now, Turle. Don't meet me at the door like that."

"Why not? How do you meet me?"

"I have to find a job. I can't pay my rent. I owe my roommate money."

"Apply for a job at the Post Office. I've always wanted to work there."

"I'm going to Yukon. It's just west of Oklahoma City." He buttoned my shirt and I put my shoe back on.

"I know where Yukon is."

"Turle, if I ever get a job somewhere, would you come with me?" He zipped my skirt and put his hands on my shoulders.

"No, Navorn."

"Why not?"

"Guthrie is where I live. I have a job here. I couldn't leave."

"Come with me, Turle."

"About the time I loved you, you'd be off to Texas. 'Good-bye Turle.' Just like my father."

"You're crying."

"Damned drifter. I might as well set my sight on the snowman."

"I can go tomorrow."

"No. I want you to go now. Isn't that what you came to tell me? What could be more important than finding work?"

"It is when you don't have it."

I pushed him out the door.

Ho twoody. I dreamed of a mahogany dust storm. Outside, the large, black rubber balloon. The noise. I heard the man with the tinsel beard open his mouth. Ki ha mo tay. I saw words move from his lips like furniture. Limbs of trees like skeletons reached for the balloon. They would rip it, but the black rubber was too thick for the fingers of the trees. The small machine used to inflate it sounded like a tractor.

I woke suddenly on the floor of my bedroom. It was the furnace in the old building. I was afraid it would erupt and send us through the sky. I would call the landlord about it again. I should call him now. Such a heavy rubber balloon in my dream. How could it fly?

CHELLY REPP

1.

    A blue shed leans into the wind. Willow-branches brush the creekbank where leaves curl like wood-shavings.

    Weeds along the ravine speak to one another: old Cherokee sisters the wind rakes together where raccoon-tracks flower the mud.

    I remember the children outside when they were young. Now he says he wants a single-bottom plow and some land. Then a mule for the blue shed.

    The last light behind us makes a halo in his few stray hairs. I wonder if he hears what I say or only what he thinks I say?

    "It's almost gone, Carl," I tell him.

    He looks at me.

    The sun yellows the grass. Wind swishes the creek-weeds and the sisters say hush to distant highway noise.

    "I see things, Carl," I say. "Soldiers crawling over our land. The ghosts of an old war-camp.

We've sold off our corners and are turning over our fields. Others will lead us."

Carl sharpens the penknife in his hand.

Somewhere, trucks line the tollgates, start across the prairie for the night, their noise trailing far behind them.

2.

"The flock of starlings in the row of river birches are like my grandfather's Cherokee hand-writing—"

"Chelly," my husband, Carl, says.

"When I had a fever of 104° I saw the soldiers. I saw food-banks. And numbers. I saw handwriting fly from the trees. And animals wearing masks."

"You aren't sick any more."

"The soldiers ran over the land cutting off our hands."

"Forget it, Chelly."

"I would, Carl, but once you've seen it—" I sigh. "You haven't been sick."

"Not like that." Carl's breath wheezes like a switch slicing the air. He sits at the table reading the paper. A man in the here and now. Cuffs of his sleeves turned back; pipe tobacco spilling from his pouch. An Indian scarf around his neck.

"I feel I'm living on the rim of the pie-pan, Carl. I want to move back to the city." I sweep under his chair. "I want to be there when it happens."

"You're not far from in the city. You can be there anytime."

"There are spirits that float around out here."

"What makes you think they aren't in the city too?"

"You said we'd only be here part of the time." I close his tobacco pouch. "You won't leave. Already you've gone from plow to tractor."

"I don't feel your discontent all the time. You sit on the porch and sketch. You water the animals—"

"They're children to me sometimes."

3.

The windmill twirls above the field like a crop duster with one propeller. The diesel tractor makes the noise of a plane engine. There are bald hills up under the sky in the distance. A silo, erect, behind the barn. Geese fly like a corner of the field-fence while night falls across the trees.

I watch Carl come back from the field. Dirt turns up waves of clouds behind the tractor. The plowed soil changes: light to dark, rolling in like a squall.

The windmill beats as though it were an old plane trying to rise from the earth. A red-tailed hawk sits on a fencepost: the wind turning up tufts of its feathers.

"We don't realize what's happening to us, Carl," I say.

"It seems to me things are stable."

"What will I do without hands?"

4.

"I miss the neighbors. The church. I don't have the women's meetings to go to. I don't have the children to draw for."

"You can drive into town—" Carl says.

"Who would make your supper? I sit on the

porch and peel potatoes while you're in the field. The church seems far away. In the next county. See how I think? I'm not close to the city anymore."

"I don't think it's the place for you, Chelly. But take an apartment there if you want."

"Away from you?"

"Just during the week when you have women's meetings at church."

"But Sundays?"

"Stay then too." He puts his hand in the pocket of my stained apron. "Then you could throw out your discontent with the potato peels."

"I don't know." I say. The cold little porch seems like a bite of Aunt Rodena's bitter torte. Water running in the next room like a tractor in the neighbor's field.

"You could stay with your younger daughter." Carl suggests.

"Our daughter," I say. "Armed with her cosmic community. What does she know?"

"We could travel after harvest," Carl tells me. "I hear the highway noise in the distance too. I could whittle and you could sketch."

"Where would we go?" I ask him.

"Indian neighbors and old pow-wows."

"Take the grandchildren?" I look at Carl.

"No."

He feels my hair and says he likes it hanging straight, not curled, like when I went to church, not in a Sunday dress and shoes. He likes the cotton dress and sweater, the curve of my stomach under the apron.

"Who would take care of the animals if we traveled?"

"Roy." He answers.

"He wouldn't care for them like we do." I say.

"Today the clouds made faces in a choir to me. See your influence?" He puts his face to my neck, his hands around to my backside.

The old farmhouse is part of everyone who lived in it. In the bedroom, a rack of rolled-up maps of Indian lands. A bureau chest. The bed. Christ in a casual pose on the wall: legs crossed at the ankle, one foot over the other, arms spread, head down, coyly almost, but for the eyes.

Mule blanket.

Muddy creek.

Chalky field-rocks like a man with a bald spot.

I kiss his head.

"I lived in the city all those years, Chelly, I have to have the farm."

5.

"What's the use of my sketches?" I look at Carl.

He glances up the road. Roy, who married the older daughter, is coming. I ask him about my drawings so Carl won't have to answer.

Roy looks through my sketches as he sits on the porch. I tell him about the striped road-barricade with the blinking yellow eye by the old bridge that reminds me of the soldiers I saw in my fever.

"We are sleeping while this goes on," I tell him. "Who will wake us?"

Roy listens to my stories. "You're the inventor, Chelly," he says.

"Carl collects old irons because he knows I don't like to iron."

"I could collect old cast-iron farm-implements now." Carl says.

I laugh. "Maybe my fever dreams are to irritate him."

"You can hardly dream up all that, Chelly," Roy says.

"My sketches of them?"

"Passable," he remarks.

I laugh again. "You are still more son-in-law than doctor."

"Probably so."

"Traffic jam," I say, making sketches, "on toast with a saucer and cup of tea. Now I saw that in a gallery by the church. Joel the prophet with fire coming out of his mouth was in a dream. AC. DC. Do you think I'm strange?"

"Sometimes, Chelly, you are." Carl says.

"I asked Roy."

"Sometimes." Roy answers.

"You're married to the only normal one of us," I tell him. "Boring as she is. My younger daughter talks new age wisdom. Carl farms. I see foreign tanks in our streets."

"Chelly, you're not making sense." Carl says and looks at Roy.

"To me I am." I look at my hands.

6.

"I think you draw just so you don't have to work in the kitchen," Carl tells me. "And you don't draw full time. You sketch."

"I take time with the animal masks for the children."

"The spare-room looks like a chicken roost. No wonder you sketch hens." Carl says. "You also have wings but don't fly. You're not here because I dragged you, but because I did what I wanted and you didn't."

"Do you have another woman?"

"No, Chelly, I have no other woman. I'm not all the way through you yet."

"I don't want to leave you."

"Why?"

"I've been your wife for forty years, trying to call silver coins from the mouths of fish."

"Maybe that's what's wrong with women. They just can't make the leap."

"We can. Yes, I'm sure we can."

"Then make it," Carl says. "You sketch with pencil, never paint. You draw your exploding world with pencil."

"My father was colorblind."

"You're not," he says.

7.

Swirling movement of the earth. Cloud-migration. The rain of birds. Mule thunder. An old log by the field-fence is a muskellunge pulled to the shore. Sometimes white birds land in the tractor's wake.

What was it men knew—Roy, Carl, that made them able to do what they wanted to?

"Kanane'ski. Amai'yehi." I hear the Cherokee sisters.

I call the animals names of children in church. I tell them "little people" stories. I talk to them about

animal transformations. I say there will be a transfer
of power. Soon I cannot tell the stories. The church
says it does not want to hear.

But the goats, mules, the cows and their calves
listen. The tractor. I have them all in masks, leading
the cow on a rope when Roy comes again.

"Curled leaves from the willow branches are
Carl's wood shavings," I tell Roy and he agrees.

The windmill sounds like a crop duster. Trucks
move across the prairie.

"The barnyard is a church to me, Roy." I tie
long strings of masks behind the fuzzy heads of the
animals, hear them pant and bray and moo.

I see the sunset in Roy's eyes.

Black and red hens in the pasture of the church.

"Naughty. Naughty." I say to one of the children when she pulls away from me. She is the
daughter that fights with her father.

"I don't know what to do now," Carl says.

"Oh Carl, let go of me. I only asked to go to
church and you said do so. I guess it wasn't the
women's meetings I missed, but the children. It's
been so long. I won't be frugal with my drawings
and masks anymore."

8.

The children bray to one another in Cherokee.
I dance with them in the churchyard by the blue
shed. They wear the masks I make. The Cherokee
sisters whisper our words. Birds handwrite them
in the river birches, lighting the church with the
barn-lantern of their language.

# FIRESTICKS

I tripped on the loose rubber footing of the bottom step when I returned from work. I went upstairs and sat in the chair by the window. Maybe I could go with Navorn if he left Guthrie. Maybe something permanent could happen now and then. I sat in the chair a long time trying to explain to myself the feelings I had. But after a while I knew I should use a hatpin to deflate whatever hope it was that bothered me.

I sat on the sofa and closed my eyes for a moment. There was the darkness of a dream again. And in that darkness, the burning firesticks the men used to carry from the holy Keetowah fire to light the smaller fires in the cabins. It had been a yearly celebration. Light out of darkness. New life from the ashes. I dreamed of the firesticks passed from generation to generation. But now we had lost our ceremonies.

Navorn slept beside me, nearly on top of me, after he came back from several days' work in

Yukon. I felt smothered, and turned toward the edge of the bed.

I saw his belongings on the floor in his partially opened duffel bag. A duck call, a cowboy hat, one spur, a .45.

"What do you need a gun for?" I asked when he woke.

"It's a pistol, lady. I take it when I travel. What time is it? I've got to get back to Yukon."

"I had another dream of the tinsel man. The man with a gray beard."

"How can I be interesting to you when you've got all that stuff going on in your head?"

"The man spoke and I saw the words come out of his mouth. Only the words were shaped like what they spoke. When he said tree, I saw a tree between his teeth. He said grass and I saw grass tumble off his tongue. He said sky and the sky flew from his lips and attached itself to the clouds. He said house and I saw four walls stand up."

"Who is it?"

"I don't know. Hope, I guess. I always felt I had nothing. Maybe it's myself speaking something into existence. Maybe words are not always separators. If I speak light I have light. My words are firesticks."

Navorn didn't say anything but I saw the red eye of his pipe he lit as he listened.

"I have to get up. I have to be at work soon too."

I went with Kay Fosher, my friend, to the Flea Market on Saturday morning in Guthrie, and then we drove to Edmond, which was just north of Oklahoma City, about sixteen miles from Guthrie, and had lunch at the Roosevelt Grill.

Marbles, Trinkets. Lamps. Comic books. Stamp collector's books. Baskets. Pipes. Pocket watches. Guitars. Hot-air balloon. A yellowed pamphlet from the BIA. A beaded leather tobacco pouch. Clay drinking vessel. Candle molds. Belt buckles.

"Kitsch." Kay said.

"Navorn, can you come over?"

"Yes."

"I tried to call you once before you answered the phone. Where were you?"

"Hasler's."

"What did you pawn?"

"The .45."

"Why?"

"I had to get my truck out of hock. I had to have work done on it and didn't have the money."

Ho twoody. Yah hoo wee. My father calls from Mount Scott. "Navorn."

"Yes."

"This is Turle."

"I knew it was."

"I want to go back."

"Where now, Turle? To Frederick?"

"No, not that far. Mount Scott, thirty miles north of Frederick."

"Why?"

"I hear my father calling from there in a dream."

"Your dreams. Hell. What does he say?"

"He doesn't say anything. I will pay for the gas.

It will be the last time."

"You said that about Frederick?"

"I didn't know I'd want to go again. Navorn?"

"Maybe."

"I want to bury his pipe and belt buckle on Mount Scott."

"When do you want to go?"

"Now."

"I miss you, Navorn, when you don't come to my apartment."

"I miss you too. I have to find more work soon. There's nothing in Guthrie. Only temporary work in Yukon. Oklahoma City never called."

"I told you that a long time ago."

"If I leave, will you come with me?"

"Where?"

"I don't know. Texas is where I was headed before I got sidetracked."

"Edward depends on me."

"So do I. Come with me for as long as we can stand one another."

"I can't, Navorn."

"You're afraid."

"I'm more afraid of the emptiness when you're gone."

"Maybe I won't have to leave."

"Yes, you will. Everything leaves."

There was a period of silence between us again as we drove. I watched the planes flying into Oklahoma City like harvesters over fields, their headlights in staggered formation in the distance, smaller and smaller, and even those I couldn't see still coming. Soon we came to Bailey Turnpike and stopped at the toll booth. I gave Navorn sixty-five cents.

"Where are you going?" I asked as he turned off on a back road near the Wichita Mountain range.

"This road is the same as any other."

"I haven't ever taken it before."

"Break away from your old habits."

"This is my country, Northerner. I should know how to get there."

"But you don't."

The Wichita Mountains sat on the flat Oklahoma prairie. Mount Scott, the highest in the small mountain range, was over two thousand feet. They looked like a distant herd of huge buffalo.

"I've been to Mount Scott before. We came here once on a trip. I think my father could have stayed on the mountain. 'Holy ground,' he said. It was where he wanted to be buried."

"Heat waves in March?" Navorn asked as we looked across the harvested cotton fields.

"Yes. You should see them shimmer in summer. The heat waves move across the land like roving tribes. My father is with them now." I rolled down the window and leaned my head into the wind.

We passed a small lake the wind plowed like a field, turning up wet rows of stubble.

A distant prairie fire made yellowish curls of smoke on the horizon.

Navorn lit his pipe.

Mount Scott was heaped with red granite boulders. A narrow road circled the mountain, which Navorn's truck climbed like a flea on the back of a buffalo. I watched the country fall below us and didn't say anything for a while. My ears popped during the steep climb.

"All events hover around us," I told Navorn presently. "White man and Indian. The murderer and murdered. O yee O. The buffalo herds pounding the prairie. Yet there was no escape, and they were slaughtered."

The wind caught the door as I opened it to get out of the truck on the top of Mount Scott. It lifted my hair. I could hear Navorn's truck hiss. He raised the hood and slammed it again. We had difficulty making our way across the parking area in the wind. We walked down through the rocks on the summit of Mount Scott, and sat for a while in the sun, away from the wind.

"Is your truck all right?"

He nodded that it was.

I watched the redbrown winter brush and the far space of prairie in the distance. The sky was like a hard, gray tarp. I thought of the mahogany faces of the rocks like people.

"My father belongs here in spirit." I dug a hole under a shrub and buried the pipe and buckle.

I felt all people again. Those who lived long lives on the prairie, and those who knew extinction of their way of life. I felt the Indians who had waited to be massacred. The artillery practice from Fort Sill on the Oklahoma prairie made an echo of the cavalry that once rode toward the small band without horses, food, guns, or protection.

The boulders on Mount Scott kept those faces before me, frozen in fear and hopelessness. A band of Indians, massacred, their blood mingled with the red Oklahoma soil.

Now I heard not only the ground thunder from the nearby army base, but also planes from the Altus Air Force base.

Hey no.

Hey yo ho yah.

Ee ho hey.

I sang an Indian chant.

I felt the ghosts that used to gather when I played in the attic of the house in Kansas City. I saw my grandmother, about to speak the language that would separate us. And I saw the dreams that gathered in my head during all those nights. Fleamarket ghosts.

Hey yey.

Eey ye hey.

The yellow smoke from a distant prairie fire made peace-smoke.

Ho twoody. There was a place to go after all. The Spirit World kept all things that left. In my vision, the prairie moved again with herds of buffalo and antelope and Indian tribes. My father rode with them, their land restored.

I remembered our early life together. It didn't matter now. Yet I felt grief that I had not known my father. That we had spent our lives apart. I saw him regret it too for a moment, when he saw me, but then all sorrow was gone from him and he rode with the tribes like heat-waves across the plains. Small white splats in the air like snow. Now I would never know him but in memory and maybe again in the time to come when I was one like them on Mount Scott, red as the soil I had tracked up the stairs to my room.

Comfort us, Great Spirit. And William Bear

Hall, my other father, I'm sorry I did not bury you on Mount Scott like you asked.

"Forgive me." The answer was his this time.

The wind was up when we left Mount Scott. The distant prairie-smoke spread across the long line of horizon.

I rode beside Navorn for a while, then laid my head in his lap and slept. But soon I sat up.

"Is that all?" Navorn asked.

"Yes."

"Why did you wake up so quickly?"

"I had my tongue between my teeth and was biting it."

"We're almost to Chickasha. Do you want a hamburger?"

Ho Twoody. Your finger in the tall grasses finds the arrow-hole in the yellow hide of the prairie. I see our words are firesticks finding a way through the dark. Strange warriors. In dreams I hear your talk.

PROVERB,
AMERICAN

It's the word, sucker. I heard it in my sleep. The word that makes things work. The stars glass the way ahead. I looked into the darkness.

Before there was anything there was word. But it stayed inside of the spirit for a while. Until that first creation point, that explosion, that was to be form. The word was so very fine I suppose you'd call it mind. It was beyond human conception. The first little bunch of stuff in the spirit was so small it was mind-word. Yep. Too fine to be energy or gross body. Just this little something. Like the stamp pin I wear on my dress. It was the first indication that something would come. It rolled around in the spirit's mouth like a tooth. It was the spirit's way of saying let there be.

Yes the spirit was everywhere and this little pet was in the bosom of the spirit and it began to roam. Yo. Up to the mouth and out. Boom.

And the word became words and they were spirit. Nobody has seen spirit. Nobody has seen word. But that's the way it was. And the word kept subdividing. It was so close to spirit it was just part of it. But it kept subdividing like I said and started forming and making firmament and everything else. Therefore the word just multiplied into words and wouldn't stop. After a while the word got so complicated it was inhabiting everywhere and had become a lot of separate things. Like mail lined up at the Post Office waiting to sort.

So at that point the unifying was the separator. A little speck that was words broken off from word. It started thinking for itself. It decided to think it was spirit and that spirit didn't really exist. Wow. The words had rebelled. They got a big head looking at everything they had done.

The words got themselves together as God and got far enough out of his house that they thought they were the house builder.

Well you can imagine all those words running loose. Words of healing. Words of laughter. Words of hurt.

 ANIMAL (TRANS) FORMATIONS

You know how people have animal counterparts. Some even fish. I knew a girl once with a long neck and a high pale head. She looked like wool and had large eyes that sat outward on her head. Everytime I looked at her I thought llama.

Her square eyes with eyelashes like postage stamps.

I think she felt it too.

She thought I would be a bird. She even said she thought she saw a feather fall from my skirt. You know the saying. Sometimes we'd talk and we'd get angry and she'd say now don't get your mandible out of shape.

We lived in a neighborhood near Tinker Air Force Base in Oklahoma City. Frieda the llama was a military brat. She'd lived over all the earth. Even out with the stars, she said. Her interstellar travelogue

was stunning. Her photo albums and souvenirs.
She was nearly all eyes as she talked. Italy. France.
Ursa minor. She was full of herstoricity. We often
made up our concepts.

If only I could see the stars.

We'll be up there on one of them someday, she'd
point to the constellations when we'd sit in the park
near our houses at night. The animals had counterparts in the stars. The Bear. The Bull. The Horse.
The Fish.

Sometimes I felt our theories waft.

I told her the stars were part of the solid rock-sky at
one time. The Native American mythologies say so.
I told her the sky rock is where we came from. But
something broke it up. Pieces of the sky rock scattered into stars.

I had her attention for once.

At one time the animals lived on the sky rock. I
fingered the carvings on the park bench. But they
started falling off. There was only water below. It
was the muskrat that dived to the bottom of the
water and brought up some mud to the surface.
There the mud grew until it became the earth we
inhabit now.

Frieda the llama spoke her different languages to
outdo me. Not all of any one of them. But parts.

Italian. French. German. Pleiadean. Well it was easy if you'd lived there.

I couldn't say languages. Not even parts. Though I'd been pentecostal once and could make something up.

I looked at Frieda's postcard on the wall. I tried to read Tintoretto's *Creazione degli Animali* in different languages. *The Creation of the Animals. Création des Animaux. Die Schöpfung der Tiere. Creación de los animales.*

In Tintoretto's painting God is barefooted, in an ankle-length dress and a shawl glowing like light. Creating the beasts. You know I'm not the first to say this. Even a dog lapping the ocean. You think we could drink it once? A rabbit with longer legs than the rabbit in my backyard has now. Another animal or mammal. A manimal. Or womanimal. With ears like two eagle feathers. Maybe God was still trying to decide you know. Still trying things out. And he took the ear feathers off the rabbit and made an eagle to put them on. Whoknows. All that light in his way. His bare feet not even touching the ground. The tire-lipped fish in the ocean. The birds flying over the water, the turkeys, and other large-bodied birds. Like those cars of the fifties with their fins. Or those square vans you see now going past Tinker on Interstate 35 like condors all over the road.

The sky full of creation too in Tintoretto's painting. Buzzards. Grouse. Pheasant. Swans. Coots and rails. They're headed west. Their engines running off the coast of Oregon, for instance, or Washington. Maybe getting ready for man. That was the order of creation when God wanted some clutter to worry about. Some grass to mow. Some hedges to trim. And then the animals. Finally us. No wonder the animals wanted to clear out.

Getting back to my friend the llama. She had long legs too and I wanted to dance with her once but we never had reason. The raison d'etre. I mean in pow-wow formation. The girls circling together. The boys in a larger circle around us. All pushing outward from that quiet center of the circle. But Frieda's center was her pumping heart.

And we argued whether we were our ideas or our ideas were us. We'd eventually fly over the hill and we had our rampant wills and ramparts parked with cars. Have you lifted the skeet-shoot of nature and seen the deer feet underneath? I asked Frieda.

I said women who wore trousers and boots could be deer.

Don't blame it on the animals she said. We both agreed the animals were a step up from us. But I said take a friendly look at nature and see what you get.

How did we ever stay together? She with her story of the universe as a moving tribe of animals stalking and scratching. The starlight sparked from the fric-

tion of their rubbing. Wasn't space frigid? She
asked. Wouldn't there be static electricity?

The sky would be one vast animal kingdom if
Frieda's theory were correct. And I could see
millions of stars through the dark of an Oklahoma
sky.

But my theory of course is that the scattered stars
are the remains of our ancient sky rock.

I looked at Frieda's postcard again. Have you turned
on? She wrote. I thought she meant the news. Well
I did one night and right there on the evening news
was the occupational army. When there was
nothing to do, terrorized animals in the captive
city's zoo. Holy Tintoretto. What viper pit were we
from? Men turned snake? Fanging the monkey. His
maimed leg held by him hissing and snarling in fear
at the camera. It was one up on us. The drafty note
from the Kuwaiti zoo after the invasion of the
foreign army. Our soldiers found the animals terrorized. Shot at. Wounded. The elephant with a bullet
in his shoulder. I suppose we'll go over there and
operate.

She would hold her thumb up to the stars if we
were sitting together in the park by our houses.
Remote and high in the Andes.

God didn't intend it that way in Tintoretto's *Crea-
zióne*. The painting on her postcard from the
Venezia–Gallerie Dell'Accademia.

When God made the fish and animals and the birds flying in the fist of the air. Los animales y anifemales. The leaping four-leggeds. Frisking up. He meant for them to be taken care of.

The animals were our responsibility.

But now there was war. And it might lead to the old explosion when the sky rock was broken up and powdered to stars. That's what the Milky Way is in my opinion. A form of powdered milk.

As Henry IV said to Hal on how to rule just keep their minds on foreign wars. So we won't see the bird within. The animal fangs. The nature's ragged slurp.

Those little bandits of our wills swiggling inside ourselves. Swinging wide from the park bench. And I said Frieda you look just like a llama. What eyelashes. What stamps licked on your lids. What lovely glassy eyeballs. God must have left them rolling around in his mouth for a while.

Over us the fireballs of planes going off.

It was even war on the animals. I would have made God with a whip frisking the animals away from us. Did God take the dust of the ground and blow his breath into them too?

I used to listen to Frieda's Broadcast of Animals on her Sunday night radio.

Bandicoots. Wallabies. Was the Indian created before Columbus? she asked. The Indian as the duckbill platypus. The go-between. The link between man and animal? No I said. The truth in my jaw snailed a signal. I think it goes the other way. We're the in-seers to the sky.

Now years later we get back to ourselves. The raisin of debt. Even plums and other berries when we had the whole land to ourselves and shared our Pez in the park just two blocks from her house. The gritty place worn clean of grass. But it reminded her of the stars she said and didn't complain.

I thought Frieda's father must be over there now. Frieda herself might be fighting the invading army who had terrorized animals in the zoo, left them hissing and bellowing with nightmares and tremors. Turned them almost into us.

What kind of salvation would there have to be to get us out of trouble? Were these the last days the llama would ask?

Imagine the animals with their mangonels behind the fortress walls at night. The language still slipping out of them. Their hands over their mouths. They gave words up you know. Animals could talk at one time too but then shut up because they wanted to give up the thing that linked them most to us.

There are times I look up in the universe at night and think it might be a ragged animal after all just ready to devour us. But then I think no we're the ones we should fear. And I return to the broken rock theory of the universe.

Speaking of space. Sometimes I see myself and Frieda out there. Along with the skunks. Spunks. Clams. Alpaca and llama. My mandible out of shape. Out there making bird-words with the blue tits. House sparrows. The common snipe.

CPSIA information can be obtained
at www.ICGtesting.com
Printed in the USA
LVHW021532120922
728171LV00004B/525

9 780806 186436